Book Three of The Deception Series
Sequel to Wrath of Deception

Will

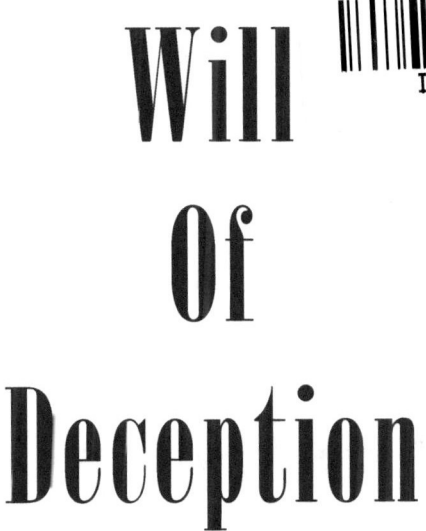

I0668279

Of

Deception

Ryan Hodge

SMP
PUBLISHING

This novel is a work of fiction. Names, places, characters, and events are either the result of the author's imagination or are used fictitiously. Any resemblance to actual people, living or deceased, places, businesses, locales or events is coincidental.

SMP Publishing Edition

Copyright © 2016 Ryan Hodge

All rights reserved. In accordance with the U.S. Copyright Act of 1976, the scanning, uploading, and electronic sharing of any part of this book without the permission of the publisher constitute unlawful piracy and theft of the author's intellectual property. If you would like to use material from the book (other than for review purposes, prior written permission must be obtained by contacting the author at contact@ryanhodgebooks.com. Thank you for your support of the author's rights.

Printed in the United States of America

10 9 8 7 6 5 4 3 2 1

ISBN: 978-0692679562 (PBK)

DEDICATION

Dear Ma,
It just isn't the same without you here,
I hold each one of our memories near and dear.
Always such a motivating and positive spirit,
Your calming reassuring voice, I can still hear it.
I'll always cherish our unbreakable bond,
Our vacations, movies, late night hangouts, I'll always
be fond.
We miss you being here in the physical sense,
You exemplified strength because you never panicked
when things got tense.
There are not enough words to accurately depict your
motherly love,
It was unearthly; it was untainted like it was created
from your new home in heaven up above.
Ma, we love you.

CHAPTER 1
Sheena's Perspective

Ilesha and Rachel both hear my words and more importantly they can see the worry, confusion, and rage that has entered my body. I release the envelope Sage handed me and I drop to the floor faster than the papers do. This is unbelievable. My girls rush to the floor to attend to me. I have a look of bewilderment on my face.

Rachel asks, "What's troubling you my sister? Are you alright?"

I say in a weak, broken voice, "The pa. The paper. Look at the paper."

Ilesha goes straight for the envelope and papers without bothering to help me up. She knows that I'm okay, but she's eager to know what knocked me off my feet. Sage stands there looking at me with a devilish grin on his face. I want to slap him into next week, but I won't because he may hit me back.

Rachel helps me up and then she reads over the papers with Ilesha. They scrutinize every inch of the papers as if they can validate or nullify their authenticity from looking at them multiple times. Rachel eventually figures something out and she smiles.

"Baby, you don't need to concern yourself with Sage's nonsense. I don't know why you follow him up. This is impossible," says Rachel.

Ilesha states, "Rachel, she didn't fall to the floor for nothing. That look on her face tells me she hasn't been forthcoming with her information. Sheena clearly hasn't told us all we need to know. Sheena, you need to share some information with us to help us better understand things."

"This is fantastic! Sheena, it seems like they don't know everything. I'll fill them in for you. Well ladies, your sister, your best friend, has been a very naughty girl," Sage comments.

"Enough Sage! You don't need to fill them in on anything. I'll tell them what they need to know. You just keep your mouth shut and let me handle this," I say.

"Okay, have at it. All this news has made me thirsty. I have to moisten my palate for I am parched," Sage comments in a pretentious tone as he leaves the room.

"Those papers are from the clinic where you had the paternity tests done. The papers indicate that Sage is the father of your sons - my godsons. I know Sage forged them," says Rachel.

"Now, there are a few different scenarios that are possible here. One is that Sage is playing his normal mind games and Eric and Kevin are the fathers of my boys. It's also possible that Sage screwed with the results and neither Kevin nor Eric is the father. Lastly, it is possible for Sage to be the father of the boys," I report.

"I knew it! By the way you fell to the damn floor. You snuck a fuck in with Sage!" Ilesha exclaims.

Rachel asks, "When did you have time to fit Sage into your schedule?"

"I know you both have a bunch of questions and I will answer them all," I say.

I explain to the girls that I had sex with Sage once right before I had sex with Kevin. The sexual encounter only lasted a few minutes. I was weak and needed to feel some dick inside of me. I didn't even have an orgasm, so it really wasn't anything to talk about. I made him stop and he didn't cum either. It was so meaningless that I honestly forgot about it. Ilesha immediately jumps on me.

"Three dicks in a short few days and two of them were new dicks. Now I hate to say it, but you're a nasty bitch. I didn't know you had that much freak in you. Hell, I want your pussy," says Ilesha.

Rachel states, "Girl, I agree with Ilesha. You need some prayer right now. You also need to slow down. You are playing a very dangerous game with all of these sexual partners. You've been very busy."

"I know. I know," I say.

"Now, if Sage didn't bust a nut, how could he get you knocked up?" asks Ilesha.

Rachel answers for me, "That's easy. He probably had some pre-ejaculatory semen that got inside of Sheena."

"Girl, why didn't you just say she got pregnant from pre-cum? Don't you know you just gave me a damn headache with that big ass phrase?" questions Ilesha.

We all chuckle from Ilesha's absurdity. I inform them that it's not likely that Sage is the father because I made him wear a condom and he never ejaculated. I tell them that anything is possible, but let's be for real, Sage is playing his normal games. I know better than to fall for them.

"Sage does play more games than a kid at summer camp, but how'd he know the clinic?" asks Rachel.

Ilesha orders, "Call his ass back in here! He has to come clean. I don't know about you two, but I'm tired of these damn games. We are getting to the bottom of this right now."

"Sage! Come here! I need to talk to you about the paternity tests results that you claim are authentic!" I shout.

Sage comes back into the living room in the same nonchalant manner in which he left. Ilesha attempts to walk over to him, but I cut her path off. There's no telling what she will do to Sage if I let her confront him. Besides, this is my conflict and I need to handle it myself. I can't keep putting my girls in the middle of things.

"I need a few things cleared up before I can halfway take you seriously," I say.

"Okay, I'll answer whatever questions you have," Sage says. "I'll grant you that much."

"So, why should I believe that you are the father of my children even though the last time we had sex you wore a condom and furthermore you didn't ejaculate?" I ask.

"That's a great question and I'm sure I'll be able to satisfy your concerns with my answers. You're right that I wore a condom, but it wasn't for the entire time. I had it on when we started, but I took it off because I wanted to feel you naturally," Sage states.

"You're an asshole! I can't believe you did some selfish and sneaky shit like that!" I yell as I lunge for him.

Fortunately for Sage, Rachel sees the anger in my eyes and grabs me before I can reach him. I know that the difference between feeling a wet vagina versus wearing a rubber is extreme, but that wasn't his decision to make. I know many men don't like to wear condoms because they claim they can't feel the woman's pussy and Sage is definitely one of those types of guys.

"You took the rubber off against my will and without me knowing, so that means I could have gotten pregnant off of your pre-cum. Thanks a whole damn lot Sage!" I reply.

Sage replies, "I didn't say it was from pre-cum. I actually bust a quick nut, but was embarrassed to tell you. That's why I pulled out and started to eat you out. That way you wouldn't question being so wet. What I'm saying is that I nutted in you."

"Sage, that was so reckless, selfish, and irresponsible of you. You really violated Sheena's wishes by doing that," says Rachel.

"You did what?!" I scream.

"I know my actions were less than commendable, but I didn't think much would come of it," Sage replies.

"Don't buy his damn apology girl! It's more Sage BS to make you feel sorry for him. I don't trust him. Everything he does is absolutely intentional and purposely done," says Ilesha.

She's right. Sage is more calculated than what he's saying. He's acting like this was an accident. Should I scream or should I go up side his head? I don't know what I should do. The idea of having Sage's baby is a thought that left my mind many years ago, but now the thought is back and is a real possibility. Ilesha is livid and hasn't stopped cursing and rolling her neck at Sage. She even tries to get at Sage physically, but Rachel holds her back.

I take a deep breath and respond, "I get it, but how do you explain knowing the clinic and getting those records changed?"

"Well, about that. I guess you didn't know, but the lab technician who did your DNA test used to work for me at the lounge and remembered you. She called me up when she saw your name along with the multiple candidates for paternity. Those both were negative, so I had her test me too and the test revealed that I'm the father," Sage narrates. "I wanted to tell you up front, but then I cowered at the idea of being a father. I made a terrible decision about how to proceed."

"Wow, is all I can say. You're really a piece of shit. I can't believe you did all of this," I say.

"I know. It all seems crazy now. I should have handled the situation way better, but I didn't and for that, I'm sorry," Sage says.

Ilesha chimes in, "I bet the hell you are sorry. We've been through hell and back behind all of these lies. I've missed out on getting fucked by my man countless times because of all of this damn deception."

"Sage, all of this lying has caused a lot of heartache. You should have been straight forward and this could have been avoided," Rachel comments.

"I know. I hoped that buying Kevin and Eric a bottle of champagne to celebrate the birth of who they thought were their sons would help make them break up with you, but you managed to keep both of them. My plan was to tell you once they broke up with you. I never expected for them to be okay with the lies you told them. I underestimated your powers. Clearly, I did," Sage replies.

"Sheena, I'm sorry, but you're taking this way too lightly. Fuck being nice and civil. He played all of us with his bullshit and what irks me more is that he put Deric and Devin in the middle of his vendetta," Ilesha comments.

Before I know it, Ilesha lunges for Sage. He attempts to get out of the way, but is unsuccessful. Ilesha knocks Sage to the floor. On the way down, Sage hits his head on the edge of his end table. He hits the floor violently and is dazed as he lies there. Ilesha mounts Sage and pulls out her blade as he rests on the floor barely conscious.

"Ilesha, take that knife from his neck now. You could kill him! It's not that serious and he's not worth going to jail for," states Rachel. "Sheena, say something to her!"

"Girl, let him up. Not that he doesn't deserve it, but you can't ruin your life for him. Let his ass up!" I order.

"I'm not letting him off the hook just like that. I'm tired of men thinking they can run over women and nothing happen to them. Hell, some shit is happening today. You aren't so slick now Sage," Ilesha voices.

Ilesha is out of control. She's pressing the knife harder against Sage's neck. It seems like the more we tell her to let him go, the more infuriated she becomes. A small stream of blood begins to form on Sage's neck where Ilesha is holding the knife. Sage is beginning to regain his composure. Ilesha slaps Sage in the face with her free hand as she continues to taunt him.

"You weak bitch. Don't play with me, my girls, or my godsons. I don't fuck around like that. You're lucky that your piece of shit ass may be the father of the boys because I could slice your throat clean through. Now, I'm gonna get up because I want to, but if you try anything while I'm getting up, I will stick your ass!" Ilesha screams.

Ilesha gets up on her own accord. Sage doesn't try to assault Ilesha as she rises off of him. Rachel cries as the blood runs down and stains Sage's shirt. I feel nothing for what has happened to Sage. I don't care about his neck or his lounge.

Sage knows that I'm very witty and a formidable adversary for anyone who challenges me. I don't play. Why would he think he could run game on me easily? I know his story is convincing, but I need to confirm his claims with a new paternity test. I may have to go to New Jersey to ensure that the test is done with the proper integrity it requires. Me and the girls leave Sage's house to begin to process this new information. We drive to In the Mix to pick up Rachel's car and then we head to a 24 hour diner to have our girl talk.

CHAPTER 2
Sheena's Perspective

My life has never been this complicated before. I feel like I'm always saying this these days. Working on my master's degree while running my business wasn't even as intricate as things are now. Every time I feel like I have finality with my situations, I get blindsided by more conflict that I have to find solutions to. When will it end?

The sole purpose of me going on a quest to find a life partner was to do exactly that - find a mate and stop having new sexual partners. Unfortunately, I've done the exact opposite and even have two children who I don't even know who their father is. Is it Eric and Kevin or only Sage? I never imagined I would be in this situation. Am I a fool for thinking a polyamorous relationship could ever work? I have to get my shit in order. I'm an emotional wreck right now.

I have to get myself together and be a better person for myself and my sons. We deserve a better me. Besides, how can I have high expectations for my sons when they get older if I'm not on point? They may look at me as if I'm a phony. Oh no, I can't and won't have that. I have to find out if Sage's accusations are true.

"Sheena, all of this worrying and crying you're doing is pointless. You'll take Sage's DNA to a lab to be tested, get the results, and go from there. Girl, no matter who the father is or fathers are, you'll still be fine," says Ilesha.

I reply, "I know. I know, but I still just wanna know. I don't like this open-ended situation. You both know my mind won't let me get past it until it's settled."

"Love, I understand. The good thing is that you don't need any of those men financially to support the boys and you have us to help you through all things," Rachel says in a calm and reassuring voice.

"You know she's right, so pull yourself together. Stop all that damn whining and get ready to face this next step," orders Ilesha.

"Girls, I'll be honest. I hope Sage is the father. Don't be mad at me," comments Rachel timidly.

"I would love to hear your rationale as to why you want that conniving and lying ass Sage to be the father of my god children," Ilesha says in a harsh tone.

"Well, it's pretty simple and sensible in my opinion. If Kevin and Eric are the fathers, then things remain complicated and messy. Let's face the facts of the situation if both of them are the fathers. There will always be public scrutiny on not just you, but the boys too when they get older. Not to mention that, you aren't currently in a relationship with Kevin or Eric," Rachel says.

"With all the bullying that's going on with kids these days, the boys would be easy targets because of the differing fathers. I get it Rachel. Not to mention, Sage is flourishing financially," responds Ilesha.

"Well, I don't know about flourishing financially now, since I had the lounge burned to a crisp. You both make good points about the benefits of Sage being the father," I say.

"The lounge was smoking worse than a forest fire. Girl, you are crazy for that one," Ilesha states.

"Yes, I agree. That was an extremely risky move. I can't believe how the smoke had filled the entire block like that," says Rachel.

Ilesha continues, "The block was so smoky that I thought we were on the set of a scary movie. Like a foggy cemetery. I could barely see my hand in front of my face. I was just waiting for the organ to start playing in the background."

My tears of worry turn into tears of laughter. I crack up laughing after Ilesha's joke. The block was very foggy from all of the smoke. Also, seeing the look on Sage's face at the fire scene makes me smile bigger than ever. The look of helplessness he had on his face was priceless.

My girls have come to the rescue again. They've turned my tumultuous sea into a calm bath. What would I do without them? I have the best friends in the entire world. They never let me down and always come through for me. When I need a base hit, they hit a home run.

"I know another reason why Sage is better off being the boys' father!" Ilesha blurts out.

"Oh really? What is that?" I immediately ask.

"Because you want him to be. That's why," Ilesha says.

I reply, "I don't know where you are coming from. Nothing about what I've said about Sage indicates that."

Rachel states, "I think you are on to something Ilesha. I was going to say the same thing when I first mentioned Sage being the best option."

"You two are both crazy. I just want my boys to be happy and safe," I say.

"The hell with all that safe talk. You can't lie to us. You know we know that Sage is the apple of your eye. You never stopped loving his dick," says Ilesha.

"More importantly, you never stopped loving him either. Sage was always your 'one' because you normally cut guys off when you stop seeing them. Surprisingly, you didn't cut Sage off," says Rachel.

"You two have been drinking too much. I'm not thinking about Sage in that regard," I say.

"Rachel, she's living in denial. She knows her ass is lying," says Ilesha.

I don't tell them, but the truth is that Sage is special to me now and always has been. I just feel complete with him. He's different from the other guys I've been with. His words, his style, and the way he treats me is second to none. There is something captivating about him that keeps me from completely walking away from him.

Sage always treated me like a queen when we were together and I was quite devastated when things went sour between us. I've always regretted our breakup. He is the man of my dreams even though he has his conniving ways. I can't be too mad about the games he plays because I often play games too.

The possibility of Sage being the boys' father is very intriguing. I hope to heaven that he is their dad. I thought he would be the one I would marry and have my kids by, but it seemed like that door had closed. Now, in the craziest of ways, at least my kids may be his. Life is an unchartered sea. No one could have predicted this series of events. I'm tickled about the future.

The likelihood that Sage isn't their dad is slim to none. He wouldn't lie about something so important for nothing. If he's lying, his lie will be revealed as soon as the DNA test results are back. He doesn't gain anything from telling falsehoods that can so easily be uncovered.

The girls and I finish our normal debrief session and I go back home and call my mom. I have to meet with her to schedule a time to pick the boys up. I'll definitely be getting a new DNA test done, but it won't be in D.C. because Sage knows too many people here. I'll have to get it done when I go to New Jersey to pick up the boys.

CHAPTER 3
Sheena's Perspective

Home sweet home! I'm so tired to the point where I really want to skip my shower and crash into bed. Unfortunately, I can't because I smell like the inside of a D.C. nightclub that I'm responsible for burning down. I've been up all night scheming and participating in felonious activities. With all that's happened and been revealed, it seems like I haven't been home in days. Hell, I can't believe that it's only been some hours. I strip down naked and rush to the shower.

As the water streams down my body, a multitude of thoughts race through my mind. Wow! I really thought I had my life planned out. I guess I was wrong. I thought burning down the club would finalize things for me, but it didn't. It actually opened up another can of worms. This hot water has a very calming effect on my body and allows me to think clearly.

I find myself smirking at the thought of Sage having impregnated me. Oh Sage - the love of my life. My first love and my first lover. It was my freshman year at Howard University and Sage's sophomore year when had our first encounter. It was totally fate in my mind and heart. I was sitting in the front of In the Mix at the bar watching a Nets' basketball game when Sage came crashing into me while escorting an unruly customer out of the lounge.

It seems like that was only yesterday. When we made eye contact and I looked into his light brown eyes, I was in love. It was truly love at first sight. I remember being a little upset because some of my drink spilled on me. Not too long later, Sage approached me in the hallway of the Blackburn Center on campus and apologized for bumping into me. He offered to take me to lunch to make it up to me and I obliged.

Freshman weren't allowed to have cars if they lived on campus, so Sage picked me up from my dorm and took me to lunch off campus. I remember being excited that an upperclassmen was showing me any attention. I remember Sage telling me that he didn't have insurance on his car. I just knew we'd get pulled over by the police and I'd have to walk back to campus. Sage told me to relax and that everything would be okay. We rode to Burger King in his silver Hyundai without being detected. I found out then that we had a lot in common and even shared some of the same goals. The craziest coincidence we learned that day is that we both are from Linden. I thought Sage was lying when told me he graduated from my alma mater. I know he's a year older than me, but I know plenty of people who graduated the year before I did, so it just seemed like I should have known him too. When I asked Ilesha and Rachel if they remembered him from school, they said they didn't recollect him either. I guess we were in our own little world.

I soon fell in love with his mind and nothing else really mattered. I later heard stories about him being a player and arrogant, but I found out from spending time with him that those rumors were not true. We dated for months without him ever asking to have sex with me. I decided if we were still dating when the end of the year gala took place, that I'd let him be my first. We were dating when the gala came and enjoyed a great night of dancing, eating, and love making. The gala was like a big party for all of the elite Howard students. When Sage came to get me in a limousine I instantly flashed back to the events before my Senior Prom. I'll never forget how I felt when we turned down McCandless Street on our way to the promenade at "The Ward". I was filled with so much excitement when the limo driver drove us to the huge crowd of people. It seemed like the entire city was there. I saw people from all sections of the town like St. Marks, Chandler World, The Ward, and DLP. We were like celebrities on the red carpet. People were taking pictures left and right like they were the paparazzi. It was definitely an experience to remember and I felt right at home in front of the cameras. However, as the evening progressed I became more and more nervous thinking about having sex with my date. I'm so glad I didn't have sex with my prom date because he turned out to be a complete asshole. I'd still be sick to this day about having sex with that guy. Fortunately, his true colors showed before the night was over and he never got to have sex with me.

Sage, however, was a total gentleman at the gala. He catered to me as if I were the only woman at the event. After the gala, we had sex and my experience was magical. He even ate me out. I really didn't know what to do. He popped my cherry and didn't even get upset when things got a little messy. He was very patient and didn't try to hurt me. He made my first time having sex very special and enjoyable. We never had any issues in our relationship even though people were often jealous and tried to intervene. Those were great times. When I went home at the end of the semester, Sage stayed in D.C. because he had to work. We even continued to date through that summer vacation and well into my junior year, but the relationship took a wrong turn. I never really got over the way things went awry. My shower is done, my eyes are heavy, and my body is fatigued. I do believe it's time for sleep.

I sleep through the remainder of the day and awaken very refreshed. It's a little after nine o'clock and I've missed many calls and texts. Eric and Kevin have both reached out to me, but I don't care about them. Deep inside the only man I want to hear from is Sage. I loved the days when we would discuss minor things, have deep conversations, or he'd just stop by to bring me flowers.

Unfortunately, Sage has not reached out to me. Maybe he's giving me time to process the news he gave me or he's probably livid about me burning down his club. If I were him, I'd never want to talk to me again. At the same time, what he attempted to do to me was extremely out of line too. I'm willing to call it even if he is. Besides, I may be the mother of his children. We have to get through it.

I know another thing that I have to get through, but I'm seriously dreading. Regrettably, I have to tell Kevin and Eric that they may not be the boys' fathers after all. Of course, I won't tell them anything until after I've gotten the paternity test taken and the results certifying that Sage is in fact their father. I don't see the point in rocking their boats before I know what's what. It could end up being unnecessary drama. We've had enough of that to last a lifetime.

Well, I guess I'll kill two birds with one stone. I have to go get the boys from my mother and I have to get the test done. I wonder if Sage would be willing to ride to New Jersey with me to take this test. I clearly can't trust any clinic in or near D.C. Sage, also known as Mr. Popularity, may have contacts in all of the clinics. I can't chance him pulling the wool over my eyes again. I decide to call Sage.

"Hey, I need to ask you something," I say after he answers the phone.

"Well hello to you too. You are straight to the point I see. So much for small talk and being cordial," Sage comments.

"Boy, please. We are years past small talk. You've seen me at my most vulnerable moments, so screw all that small talk. Besides, I don't have the luxury of wasting time on minutia," I reply sharply.

"Ouch! Take my head off why don't you? I'm just saying we can be friendly and not be short with one another. I'm not holding any grudges. I did what I did and I got what I got. That's karma," Sage says.

Sage is definitely the type of person who will seek revenge if he feels he has been wronged, but he's also the type of person who takes his lumps like a man. He won't complain or hold any grudges when things fall back on him. For example, he hasn't mentioned me burning down the lounge one time. He took his loss gracefully.

"Okay, we can be cordial. I'm not mad at you either. We're even-steven in my book. I called to see when we can get this paternity issue resolved," I say.

"I understand why you want to get your own test performed. I wouldn't trust me either with all the back and forth you've had lately. I'm at your disposal, so you just let me know when," Sage says.

I reply, "I'd like to have this settled sooner rather than later, so I called and scheduled it for Saturday."

Sage replies, "I agree. I'm ready to assume my role as Deric's and Devin's father, so the sooner the better. I can meet you whenever."

"Thanks, that's great, but slow down with all that assuming your role stuff. We'll discuss all of that after the paternity results come back. Well, I don't trust any clinic in the area after your stunt, so we will have to go to Linden to get it done," I state.

"You wanna go all the way to Jersey to get it done?" Sage asks.

"I most certainly do. Besides, I have to pick the boys up, so it just makes sense to do both at the same time. It'll be a good weekend trip for you," I remark.

"Shoot, I haven't been home in too long anyway and resolving this is urgent, so let's get it done. I'll take the road trip," says Sage.

"K. We can leave early Friday morning," I say.

Sage agrees to meet me at my house on Friday morning. I tell him that we will leave at six in the morning, so we can get there early and have enough time to spend with family and friends. We won't have to rush and can even stop to eat if we need to. It will undoubtedly be a very long week while I wait for Friday.

My girls are giving Sage credit for being so flexible about going to Jersey to have the paternity test done. A lot of men would have bitched and moaned about being so inconvenienced, but not Sage, he suited right up. I give him some credit for that. It seems like he wants to make this process as smooth as possible. I really don't know if I can handle any more chaos. I've had more than my share of it lately. I get my clothes out for work and iron them. After I iron my clothes, I get back in the bed and fall asleep.

CHAPTER 4
Sheena's Perspective

It's time to rise and shine already. I'm up early and well rested. I needed that full day of rest to get my body back in order. I get myself together and head to work. While I'm driving to work, I receive a good morning text from Eric. I really don't want to text him back, but I do. I keep the message short and only reply with "GM".

Eric asks me what I'm doing for lunch and tells me that he wants to meet up if possible. I don't have any plans for lunch, so I decide to indulge him. I'm actually surprised he wants to do lunch. Our last encounter wasn't the most pleasant. He was extremely upset seeing Sage leave my place in the middle of the night. Maybe he'll have something worthwhile to talk about. I arrive at work to plenty of emails to respond to and fires to put out. I'm not complaining about being busy because being busy indicates that I have clients. Having clients, pays the bills.

The phone hasn't stopped ringing either. The life of a financial consultant is very demanding. My clients are always heavily involved with their money and I don't blame them. I think the only thing that's more important to people than their money is their kids. Most people don't even monitor their health the way they monitor their assets.

After hours of hustling and bustling, the madness finally quells a bit. It's great timing that things have now calmed down because I'm starving. Let me switch gears from professional Sheena to personal Sheena, so I can deal with Eric for lunch. I hope he doesn't want to argue. Let this meeting be a friendly one because I'm not carrying any ill vibes back into work. There's way too much time left in the work day to be aggravated.

Eric sends me a text to let me know that he's outside. I run to the restroom to straighten my hair up. I'm sure it's a little disheveled after the morning I've had. Eric's not on my favorite person list right now, but I still won't let him see me without having myself on ten. I give myself a final check and head out to his car.

Eric is standing at the passenger's door and opens it for me. I sit in the car and he closes the door behind me. This is a total reversal from how he was acting the other night. Is this some sort of setup? Setup or not, I'll play along with it. I'd rather have peace than war. Eric gets in the car and hands me a card that he has sitting in his sun visor. I neglect to read the card in front of him.

"Thanks for accepting my lunch invitation. I wasn't sure if you would because of the way things ended the other night," Eric says.

"Things did get a little out of hand the other night, but there aren't any hard feelings on my part. I just couldn't understand why you couldn't understand that I needed to go. It was late and things were happening that needed to be handled," I say.

"I get it now. I see that the lounge burned down, so it makes sense as to why you had to go," Eric says.

The truth is, he doesn't know why I had to go. I think he told himself that I had to go because the lounge caught fire to make himself feel better about me pulling off on him the other night when he popped up. It's amazing how people come up with stories to justify their own actions. In some cases people make themselves see things they didn't really see or say they don't know what they really do know.

I remember one time in high school a good friend of mine saw her boyfriend draped all over another girl and managed to convince herself that she didn't see what she really saw. That's one hell of a defense mechanism. Denial must make the pain of reality hurt less. I don't mind Eric making excuses for me because his excuses are keeping the peace between him and me.

I reply, "Yes, I was just trying to help a friend navigate through a very chaotic and trying time. I would want somebody to help me out if I were to face such atrocities. We have to help each other heal through prayer and empathy," I narrate.

I'm really just babbling to go along with Eric. I don't care about Sage's lounge one bit. It's gone and it's not coming back. Eric agrees with me about helping people in need. He even tells me that he is in need.

"What are you in need of?" I ask.

Eric replies, "I'm in need of love, so what about us?"

"That's cute. Jodeci. I remember that song," I say.

"It's one of my favorites. On a serious note, I really do miss you. I haven't seen much of you lately, so I've been a bit frustrated. So when I saw Sage there the other night, I lost it. I was way off base," Eric explains.

I state, "I totally agree. You violated me on so many levels. You popped up unexpectedly, you questioned me even though we weren't an item, and became upset with me."

"I know. I was emotionally unstable. I apologize from the bottom of my being," Eric states.

"I accept your apology. I understand you're going through some things. Hell, I am too. You still have to keep your emotions in check. It's better for all of us moving forward," I reply.

"Agreed. I think I've been so edgy lately because I miss seeing my son. On top of that, I haven't had your sexual healing since I don't know when," narrates Eric.

I really understand where he's coming from because I have been nixing him off a lot lately. He really hasn't done anything to me for me to have treated him so poorly. I really intended to be with him exclusively after he and Kevin first fought. Unfortunately, he rubbed me the wrong way when he came to my house in the middle of the night. Now, I'm unsure about our future together. Once, I know for sure that Deric really isn't his son, the relationship is over. I will cut his ass off faster than split ends on my hair.

"Hey, I know what you mean about missing Deric. I can't wait to see him and his brother. I'm going to get the boys from Linden on Friday," I say.

"Oh really? What time are you planning on going to Linden? I'd love to go with you. I'll even do all the driving, pay for gas, and we can drive my car," says Eric.

"Sorry. You can't go with me this time. I'm already riding with somebody who's going to take care of all of the driving. Thanks. Next time I'll be sure to take you up on your offer," I state.

"Oh, I understand. You don't want me to infringe upon your girl time, huh? I wouldn't fit in with all you ladies riding in the car. I guess that would be a little awkward. You ladies won't be able to talk about the things you want to talk about. I get it, really I get it, forget that I asked," Eric responds.

I reply, "No honey. I'm not riding with the girls. Actually, Sage is riding to Jersey with me. We have some business to handle while we're up there."

"Wait. Wait. You mean to tell me that Sage is driving you to Jersey to pick up my son. You gotta be kidding me. Here it is I'm trying to make amends with you and understand where you're coming from, but you're parading around town with Sage. I really can't believe you," Eric replies angrily.

I reply, "Eric, it's really not what you think. It really is business and I need you to understand that. I'll explain it to you later when I return, but business is business."

"Damn all that! I'm tired of you taking my kindness for weakness. You must really think I'm some type of joke, don't you? Well, I'm not. And if you know better, you won't have Sage take you to Jersey and get in the car with my son. I don't want him around my boy," Eric narrates.

"I hear you. Fortunately, you don't tell me what to do. In fact, the last time I checked, I govern myself. Not you, not Kevin, or anybody else. So what you can do is stop acting like you own me and telling me what to do. I trust Sage around my sons, so that's all I'm going to say about this," I dictate.

"See, this is exactly what I'm talking about. You don't treat me like I'm a real man. You don't treat me like I can have a say so in my son's life. Well, I can and I will. You need to start respecting me as a man," Eric comments.

I grab my stomach as if I'm in pain. I lean forward and tell Eric to stop the car. Before he has a chance to stop the car, I roll down the window to get some air. Eric doesn't have a safe place to pull over just yet, so he drives a little bit further. Once he gets to a safe location, he begins to pull over.

"Sheena what's wrong?" Eric asks in an extremely panicked voice.

"I think I'm going to be sick," I reply as I get out of the car.

Eric immediately jumps out of the car and runs to the passenger's side. He has genuine concern about my welfare in his heart. I really appreciate that, but I don't appreciate his attitude. He needs to just go along with what I'm saying and not be such a bug-a-boo.

"What's making you sick? Is it something you ate?" Eric questions.

I reply, "No, it's not something I ate. It's you always whining like a little ass girl that's making me sick. You're turning my stomach and it's disgusting. I need you to be more like a man and stop being so sweet. All that sweetness is making me nauseous. I had to get out of the car to end it. I'd rather be water boarded than to keep hearing all of that complaining. It's torture."

"You are freaking unbelievable. You seem to think that life is all about Sheena. Sheena, Sheena, Sheena. Well, guess what? It's not. People have feelings and you can't just walk over everyone when you feel like it. I'm just telling you how I feel. And I feel disrespected," Eric states.

I reply, "And I feel the urge to throw up. I'm not getting back in the car with you if you keep on whining and complaining. I just don't feel like it. I just can't take it anymore."

"Sheena, get your ass back in the damn car. You'll listen for as long as I need to talk," says Eric.

I say, "I will not get back in the car with you. I don't have to listen to you complain and I damn sure don't have to listen to you give me orders. I keep trying to tell you I'm my own woman and I do my own thing. As far as I'm concerned, you can drive your ass out of here. I'll be fine. In fact, I'm calling Uber now."

"Fine, the choice is yours. I don't care if you don't want to get back in the car with me. It's your world, right Sheena? The world is yours and it's your prerogative to do whatever you want in it. And if you're dumb enough to walk or call Uber, that's fine with me," Eric says.

I don't respond to Eric. I walk down the street to McDonald's and grab a salad. The driver is on his way. Eric pulled off and I don't see his car anymore, so hopefully he's not coming back around to check on me. I really just couldn't take any more of his foolishness. I was just trying to have a nice lunch and not be bothered. I should have known Eric couldn't let it be that simple because he's overly emotional.

I chose not to lie to him about who was driving with me to New Jersey. As they say, the truth shall set you free. I want to be free because I'm tired of hiding and lying. I have to get right with myself, so I can be right with my boys. I'm extremely surprised that Eric actually left me. Maybe he does have a set of balls in those pants of his. It's about damn time. I can't stand a weak man. In fact, I can't stand anyone who will allow someone to walk over them.

The Uber driver shows up shortly after I get my salad. I ride back to my job and enjoy my lunch at my desk. At least now, I don't have to entertain anyone. It's just me and my office. Tranquility is a beautiful thing and I appreciate it. While I'm eating, I receive many text messages from Eric calling me many names that really I don't like to be called, but I don't let it bother me. He's extremely irate. I think he's really just a jealous man who's not getting his way. A man who doesn't get his way is a big baby and I'm not going to be his pacifier.

I jump right back into my work as soon as I finish my salad. Absorbing myself in work is the only way I'll be able to forget about Eric and his nonsense today. If I don't distract myself, I'll just think of ways I could have done more or something that I could have said to really get under his skin. I'll overthink this scenario 20 million different times.

Finally, Eric stops calling and texting my phone. Now, I can truly focus on my work and get this workday behind me. It has been hectic to say the least. I text the girls in a group chat to fill them in on Eric's shenanigans this afternoon. Ilesha bashes him like always and calls him all sorts of derogatory terms. Of course Rachel wants us to see how emotional he is and how it's causing him to act out. She says that we should not judge him, although she doesn't agree with him cursing at me. Additionally, Rachel doesn't agree with me getting out of his car and catching the Uber to my job. She feels it was a dangerous move on my part and that I should be more responsible in securing my safety. I totally understand where my sister is coming from. She has my well-being at heart and I'll never fault her for that. That's one of the reasons why I love her so much. While I'm texting them, I receive a text from Kevin. I open the text message to see what it says.

Kevin texts, *"What's this I'm hearing about you going to New Jersey to pick up Deric and Devin with Sage?"*

I text back, *"Sounds like you've been talking to Eric. You have heard correctly. Sage and I are traveling to New Jersey to take care of some business and yes I will be picking up the boys and bringing them back to D.C."*

Kevin replies, *"That doesn't sound like a good idea to me. If you need someone to take the drive with you to pick up my son, I'll be more than happy to make it happen. This Sage business is out of the question."*

I send him a text back that reads, *"I did not ask you to take the ride with me. I told you what I'm doing and that's what I'm doing. I need you and Eric to mind your business on this one. It has nothing to do with you or him. I'm not in a relationship with either of you and don't feel the need to proceed as if I am and listen to your wishes."*

Kevin promptly texts me back, *"I burned down that bastard's lounge for you. I thought that we'd be together after I did that. Now you are going to New Jersey with him like you two are an item. I'm confused and angry because it seems like I did that for nothing. Now, I did want to get some revenge on Sage for myself, so I'm not too mad about that, but I don't like the idea of him being around my child. I don't trust him and unless you want something to happen to him similar to the lounge, you'll tell him he can't take the road trip with you. Sheena, just know that I'm not playing with you or him damn it!!!"*

I decide to play dumb when he mentions burning the lounge down. I know better than to put that type of information in a text message. He'll probably try to get me locked up or something. I may have been born at night, but it wasn't last night, so I won't even confirm that part of his message. Also, it really seems like he's threatening Sage's life in this text. I guess if he was violent enough to burn down Sage's lounge, even though he got help from me, I should take him seriously on his threat.

I text back, *"You seem upset like always. I need you to calm down and not make threats. It's really not that serious. No one needs to get hurt here. We are all adults and we can act like it. With that being said, I am going to New Jersey with Sage. The boys will be back soon and you can see them then."*

Kevin continues to rant and curse in his text messages. Fortunately, I have to conduct an employee meeting, so I don't engage any of his text messages for a while. Once he realizes that I'm not responding, he stops sending text messages. It amazes me how a man can be extremely well spoken, but when he gets emotional, all of his oratory skills go out the window and he reduces himself to a person with a low lexicon level. He doesn't know how ignorant he sounds by hurling curse words back and forth.

I finally have a moment to text Kevin back. He has sent multiple text messages that are very long. I know he's expecting me to text him back just as long of a message that he has sent me, but

I don't want to give him too much to engage. I decide to text him back very short answers to his text messages. For example, I respond to one of his messages with "K". I also respond to another one of his other messages with the word "Yeah". I know the short text messages are driving him insane, but I feel like messing with him since he's disturbing my workday. I didn't instigate his verbal assault. Eventually, the day ends and I leave work to go home and prepare for the next day.

CHAPTER 5
Sheena's Perspective

It's Friday morning and it's time to go pick my boys up. I'm so excited. I miss my adorable kings so much. I'm not going to be able to stop hugging and kissing them. Sage will be here shortly, so I need to hurry up. I know he won't be a moment late. I'm surely not putting on an outfit that's overly cute. I don't want Sage to think I'm trying to impress him. On top of that, I want to be comfortable for the ride.

As soon as I step out of the shower, my doorbell rings. Damn, Sage is early. He'll just have to wait outside for a little while. Hell, it's not my fault that he's early. What's the point in setting a time if you're going to show up when you want to anyway?

I glance at my phone to see what time it is. To my surprise, it's actually after six o'clock. I can't believe that I'm the one who's late! That shower was feeling so good that it had me lose track of the time. He's already called twice and texted once. I decide that it's only right to go let him in. I'm wrapped in my towel and still wet from the shower when I open the door.

As I open the door I say, "Sage, I'm so sorry for losing track of the time."

"I don't mind, especially since you let me see you slightly wet and in a very skimpy towel. If this is what will happen when you're late, feel free to keep being tardy. Besides, I've overslept before and it is pretty early," Sage states with a smirk on his face.

"Very funny, but all you'll be seeing is me in this towel. Don't get any ideas. You're lucky to see this much skin," I say.

"I know. Lucky me, but seeing you like this reminds me of how your hair and body would be a little sweaty after we made love," comments Sage.

"Boy please! Don't try to reminisce with me about sex. I know you Sage. You are always up to something. Don't think this trip means that I like you because I don't. This is strictly business for me. You taking this trip with me can provide me with the answers I seek. Nothing more and nothing less," I remark.

"Darling, I have no ulterior motives here. I only wish for the truth to be brought to light from this road trip. I know the truth and you'll soon know what I know. This has been a long time coming," says Sage.

I reply, "I'm not your darling, so don't refer to me as such. You forfeited your pet name privileges a long time ago. I suggest you stick to calling me Sheena. That's best for our current situation."

"Okay Ms. Mills. I'll be sure to keep the drive completely professional. I don't want to act like we've known each other for years and we've had sex before," Sage says sarcastically.

"You can be as sarcastic as you like, but that's the past and today we're dealing professionally," I say.

"Why do you act like you're so hard when I know the true you? Don't you know you can't fool me?" Sage asks.

"I'm hardened inside. I used to be sweet, but I'm different now. The games men play have changed me. I will no longer accept the role of the victim," I reply.

"That must be why you victimized me. I guess it's some sort of a defense mechanism or something," Sage remarks.

"Well, I've learned from men that it's eat or be eaten. As they say, survival of the fittest," I say.

Sage is the person who taught me the rule to protect myself. Our relationship taught me how being vulnerable and head over heels for someone doesn't always pay off. Our breakup really took a toll on me. I've always regretted the way things went. Sage really was insensitive to my feelings and I still remember it vividly.

It was during my junior year and his senior year of college when we broke up. I was busy trying to ensure that my senior year would be a success and really couldn't give Sage the time he wanted. In some instances he would be free, but I wouldn't be. Our schedules weren't on the same page, so Sage became discouraged and broke things off with me.

Additionally, he complained of being sexually frustrated. I knew he had a high sex drive, but I felt he could have sacrificed for me. He knew that I had a rigorous schedule and I wasn't neglecting him on purpose. I didn't want to part ways, but I had no choice but to go along with his decision. It's not like I was going to stalk him or anything.

We continued to communicate regularly after the breakup. Sage was like a special best friend. That all changed when my travel plans changed during spring break. I had already left D.C. for the break, but once my plans got canceled, I decided to go back to D.C. and spend time with Sage. I didn't want to tip Sage off, so I didn't tell him that I was coming.

I asked, "Sage, are you going to be free during spring break?"

He responded, "Yeah, I'll be around. I'll probably work a few hours at In the Mix, but other than that, I'll be chilling."

"Okay, sounds pretty laid back. You should take it easy, during your break," I said.

"Yeah, I plan to do just that," Sage replied.

I had the our time together all planned out. I figured Sage and I would do some shopping, catch a movie, and do some sightseeing just to name a few things. I even planned to give him some of my goods. Clearly, Sage had other plans. When I arrived on Howard University's campus, I called Sage to see where he was. Unfortunately, he didn't answer his phone. I waited on campus at the Blackburn Center for Sage to hit me back, but he was taking forever.

A bright idea popped into my head while I waited. Something told me to go to his dorm room because he may be in there sleeping. The only problem was that I really wasn't a fan of popping up at someone's residence unannounced.

I walked over to Drew Hall where Sage was living. I had no way of getting in the building, so I stood outside for a moment and waited for someone to either go in or come out. Luck was on my side because a girl came walking out of the dorm.

"Hey, can you hold the door for me?" I asked.

I thanked the girl and proceeded to Sage's dorm room. I called Sage and sent him a text to alert him that I was on my way to his room, but again he did not respond.

I walked to the door and saw a picture of Sage taped to the door like normal, but there was a sock tied around the door handle. I had seen plenty of college movies to know what that meant. I became infuriated and jealous at the thought of Sage in there fucking some other female.

My anger took over and I began to pound on the door. I was really tripping because I could hear the bed constantly bumping against the wall. They didn't even stop having sex when they heard me beating down the door. I really lost it when I heard the girl screaming. I started kicking the door at that point.

I was fully prepared to kick the door off its hinges. I was making a huge scene in the hallway, but I didn't care. A few people peeked out of their rooms to see what was going on. Many of them thought it was funny and began to laugh. Finally, the door opened and a very attractive girl exited the room hesitantly.

"Bitch, who are you and where is Sage?" I asked angrily.

"Bitch, who you calling a bitch? Do you know who I am?" she asked.

As soon as I heard her call me a bitch, I got one good slap square across her face before I saw a dude coming out behind her. In the same instance, I got grabbed from behind. It was Sage grabbing me and pulling me away from the girl. The guy who was in the room wasn't Sage. Apparently, he let his friend use his room. Fortunately, his friend grabbed the girl I slapped and kept her from hitting me back.

Sage cursed me out ten different ways. I knew I was wrong for what I did, but Sage was wrong for talking to me like that. He berated me like a child in front of everyone in the hallway. I was so embarrassed. To make things worse, Sage had plans to go out with a female he's been into and refused to cancel the date with her for me.

"Sheena, I'm not canceling my date with Monique to make you feel better. I never told you to come down here anyway. I don't know what to tell you, but you aren't staying with me tonight. Monique is spending the night with me," said Sage.

"Really? That's how you're going to do me? What do you expect me to do for the rest of the night?" I asked.

Sage said, "I really don't give a fuck where you go. Take your ass back to your dorm or go home if you want. All I know is that I'm spending the night with Monique."

I had never felt so played in my life. I couldn't believe Sage would pick some side chick over me. Our relationship was never the same after that. He treated me badly for a piece of pussy.

I finally get dressed and pack my bag for the road. We are ready to go. Sage carries my bag to the garage for me. He throws my bag in the trunk and then walks over to his car to get his overnight bag. As I back out of the garage, I see Kevin and Eric approaching Sage at the trunk of his car. What the hell are they doing over here? What the hell are they about to do to Sage?

Sage has his back to them, so I press the horn as fast and as hard as I can. Sage picks his head up, but it's too late. Kevin and Eric are both right on him. I should have let Eric think I was traveling with the girls and maybe Sage wouldn't be cornered right now.

I'm just tired of lying and hiding from people. I had far less problems when I was on the up and up. I guess there is such a thing as being too honest. I know one thing, if they hurt Sage, I'll be sick to my stomach. His injuries would be entirely my fault. I know he can fight, but he surely can't take on both of them.

What would my girls do? Ilesha would jump out and fight, while Rachel would stay safe and call the police. I don't have enough time to call the police before it goes down. I guess I'll have to jump out of the car and see if I can quell the situation. Hell, three men standing face to face may not be any place for a woman.

I run over to them. I can't believe I'm standing with three men who I've had sex with. My life is unreal. Sage stands before them, but doesn't seem worried, but I think he should be because Eric and Kevin are both filled with rage.

"Sage, you're not going anywhere with Sheena that involves my son," says Eric.

Kevin replies, "Yeah, I agree. We've had our issues before this, so I think it'll be inappropriate for you to be in my son's presence. You seem to be educated, so you should understand where I'm coming from."

"I can understand you guys not wanting me around your sons. I get it. I wouldn't want certain people around my kids either," Sage says.

"I'm glad you see where we're coming from," Kevin says.

Sage replies, "Totally, but about your sons."

I interrupt Sage because I know he's about to tell Eric and Kevin that the boys are his. They will pummel Sage for sure if he says that. They want to cause him bodily harm just for being around the boys. I can't even imagine what Sage claiming them as his kids would bring about.

"Enough is enough. There is too much violence in this world. Just walk away from one another. This is just too much. I can't keep doing all this fighting in the streets," I say.

I connect with the correct brain cells with Eric and Kevin because they both back up from Sage. Sage closes his trunk and walks toward my car. Using the key fob, I pop the trunk again, so he can throw his bag inside. I walk back to my car and get in. Sage proceeds to open the driver's side door, so we can leave.

Kevin screams, "Oh, hell no!"

Kevin is clearly livid because he realizes that Sage is intent on going to Jersey with me. Sage sits in the seat, but before he can close the door, Eric holds it open and Kevin reaches in to grab Sage. They all engage in a scuffle. Blows are flying left and right and I scream for them to end the madness. Sage kicks Kevin and then Eric punches Sage in the face. The punches are being so wildly thrown that Kevin and Eric even hit each other a couple of times.

Sage eventually ducks his head. It looks like he's covering up. The blows must be taking a toll on him. He eventually returns from the tucked position. To my horror, the next thing I hear is the staccato sound of a gun being fired. The pop of the gun being fired silences the noise of the brawl. I think I've just aged ten years in a split second.

It's apparent that Sage did not tuck to hide from being hit. He reached down to pull his pistol from his ankle strap. Kevin and Eric both fall to the ground after the shot. Since they both fell, I don't know who's hit. Sage is still holding the gun in his hand and jumps out of the driver's seat.

"Don't move!" Sage commands.

Kevin and Eric are both still on the ground. Sage points his gun at them. I get out of the car to see which one of them is shot. Also, I want to convince Sage not to kill them. They are idiots, but they don't deserve to die. When I get to the spot where Kevin and Eric are, I see blood on Kevin's shirt. I have to call 911.

I say, "Don't shoot! Don't kill them. You'll throw away your future. They aren't worth it."

Sage sternly replies, "Sheena! Move out of the way now! And I mean right now!"

I've never seen a more serious look in his eyes before and never heard his voice so calm and controlled. My intuition tells me that I better listen. I don't want to end up shot too. I hope Kevin doesn't bleed to death. The authorities may want to charge me as an accessory to this crime if Kevin dies. I can't have that.

"Sage, I'm calling an ambulance. Kevin needs to get to a doctor before he bleeds to death," I say.

"He's not going to bleed to death because I didn't shoot him. That was a warning shot. Kevin is bleeding on his shirt from his nose being busted," says Sage.

I didn't know. I heard the gunshot and saw them fall to the ground. They tripped over each other when they attempted to flee after hearing the shot. Sage calmly addresses Kevin and Eric.

"Fellas, that was a warning shot. I really could have shot and killed both of you, but I chose not to. If you attempt to physically assault me again, the next shots will be fatal. I promise you that. We are going to leave now, but I will not be so forgiving if there is a next time," Sage dictates.

Sage tells me to get in the car, while he still has the guys at gunpoint. They don't make a move. Sage gets back in the car and closes the door. We pull off without further incident. I'm glad no one was seriously hurt, but I'm a nervous wreck. I almost broke down back there. I've been around some serious situations before, but I've never been this close to a shooting and I'm not looking forward to it ever happening again.

I'm so shaken that the only thing that will calm my nerves is a drink. I can't even tell Sage to go back to my house because I don't want to bump back into Kevin and Eric. There's no telling how long they'll be outside of my house. Additionally, I wish I could suggest to Sage that we run by In the Mix for a drink, but I can't because I helped burn it down. I guess I'll have to wait to see my boys to gain a sense of calmness.

CHAPTER 6
Sheena's Perspective

We are well into the drive traveling up I-95 and Sage is cool, calm, and collected. You would think that he wasn't just attacked and that he didn't just fire his gun. How could someone be so calm after something so dramatic? To the contrary of Sage, I'm still a nervous wreck. I can't stop shaking or crying. Tears won't stop streaming down my face.

I've never been in any situation that even came close to anything like what happened today. What if he would have shot Kevin or Eric? Even worse, what if I would've been shot? Fights, guns, and gunshots have become a part of my life. This entire situation is extremely out of control. Once this DNA test is taken and the results are confirmed, I'll be certain to put my life back in order. I'll be like Mary J. Blige because

I'll have no more drama. Sage notices how shaken I am and pulls the car over at a rest stop. We sit in the car and converse.

"Sheena, are you going to be okay?" Sage asks.

"I guess I will be. My mind is just racing rapidly and my nerves are shot. I can't stop shaking," I reply.

Sage replies as he rubs my arm to calm me down, "Yeah, things got way out of hand back there. I'm sorry it went that far. I only use my gun as an absolute last resort. I felt I had no choice given the situation. I hate that you had to see that. I've carried my pistol ever since I got shot at the lounge. I told myself from that day forward that I'd never be the victim again. Unfortunately, I still remember it like it happened earlier today. I was sitting in my office filling out some paperwork and looking over some delivery order forms when I heard someone come into the lounge. It was strange that someone came in the lounge because it was early Sunday morning and we were closed at the time. Before I had a chance to get up and investigate, the assailant was in my office holding a gun with it pointed at me. I asked the mystery man what he wanted because I figured it was a robbery. I couldn't figure out what else the person could have wanted. Thinking that the person wanted to rob me is exactly what saved my life. I say that because the person who shot me pulled the trigger without saying anything. Since I thought it was a robbery, I leaned over slightly to reach in my back pocket to grab my wallet and throw it to the person. That was the same moment the person pulled the trigger while aiming right for my head. Instead of the bullet hitting me in the head, I was hit in the shoulder. That subtle movement was the difference between me being alive today instead of dead."

Sheena, there was blood everywhere. My clothes were blood soaked and so was my desk and floor. I thought I was going to die. I recall vividly how hot the bullet was as it entered my body. I know I lost consciousness for a while, but fortunately when I came to, the person was gone. I crawled to my phone and called 911. The next thing I knew I was at the hospital with you by my side and the cops asking me a bunch of questions. You were there for me when I was at a very low point in my life."

"You don't have to apologize for what you did. Eric and Kevin were way out of line. They never should have attacked you. I'm all for self-defense. They really had whatever happened to them coming. I totally don't blame you," I say. "Honestly, I should be apologizing to you. I should have never told Eric we were heading to Jersey together. Those two lunatics probably sat outside my house all night long. I'm surprised you finally told me about that day you got shot. You're normally so closed mouth about the shooting that I thought you'd never open up about it. I'm glad you confided in me."

"Okay, great. I really don't want you to be upset with me. I hope we can put the bad times behind us and move forward. I told you because I don't want you to think I'm some type of bad person for shooting at them," Sage comments.

"I hope we can too, but we'll see about that Sage. You make it hard for me to trust you because of all of the tricks up your sleeve. I know you only shot to protect yourself and I don't think you're a psycho," I state.

"I have a trick or two up my sleeve, but you have several tricks yourself. You know we were a great tandem when we were a couple. We were always clicking on the same cylinders. We could finish each other's statements like we were reading from the same script. I miss those times and I miss you," Sage says.

I pronounce, "Hell, you sure have a funny way of showing it. Seems like you enjoy being with yourself more than you do with me."

When I graduated high school, I attended Howard University like Sage did. Although I went to Howard University after Sage, my decision to attend that University had nothing to do with him. I wanted to attend Howard University from the first time I stepped on campus. Mr. Brooks, Ilesha's dad, took us on a road trip to visit the campus and I fell in love with Howard University's business school and I wasn't going to let anything preclude me from accomplishing my dream.

Honestly, I was beyond happy that Sage was at Howard University when I got there. Even though Sage and I had some rocky roads, I never could quite get over him. He took my virginity and I always hold him in high regard. I guess it's a curse. I had sex with him with no strings attached throughout the rest of my college career because I hoped it would lead to us getting back together. My plan to get him back almost worked too. Unfortunately, when he became heavily involved with In the Mix, things went awry yet again. Sage began meeting a lot of women and distanced himself from me to be free to have sex with whomever he wanted. I was hurt by a man who I had deep feelings for. It was hard to cope with the disappointment. I was only able to get through it because my girls afforded me unwavering support.

"I know it looks like I'm just babbling and running my mouth, but I really do miss our times together. It's hard for you to believe me and I get it. I get it, but you've always been the one who holds a special place in my heart. You're the only woman who has ever floated my boat," Sage utters.

"So, why all of the inconsistent behavior? Why not just make me yours and be done with it? Why keep playing with my emotions?" I ask.

"In a funny way, I behaved the way I did because I didn't want to lose you. If I would have made you mine, I probably would have cheated on you because my mind wasn't where it needed to be. I was immature, but I know you well enough to know that if I would've cheated on you, you never would have forgiven me for that. I respect you too much to have done that," Sage recites.

This is why I'm always so conflicted when it comes to my dealings with Sage. I can't stay mad at him for long because the wrong that he does always has a reason to justify it. My girls haven't liked Sage for years because of his treatment of me.

"You're right about that. I woulda never spoken to you again for cheating on me. I don't tolerate being cheated on, so consider yourself lucky for not going that route," I vocalize.

Sage remarks, "It wasn't luck that I never cheated on you, it's respect that kept me from doing so."

"Aww, that's so sweet. You can be a good man when you want to be. I guess I can't be too mad that you have your ways because I have my ways too," I say.

"When I heard you were engaged, I was sick to my stomach. I thought my chance of being with you was lost forever. Miss, I thought back to the time we danced together at your cousin's wedding. That day, I pictured you and me dancing at our own wedding. I was kicking myself because I thought I lost you because I was being foolish," Sage orates.

We were clearly thinking the same thoughts because I had the same premonitions that day. We danced, talked, and laughed the entire time. It was a perfect day and I'll cherish it forever. My nerves have calmed down tremendously. Sage reminiscing has taken my thoughts off of the fight at my house. He's still rubbing my arm in an attempt to calm me down, but what he doesn't know is that he's now turning me on. My natural reaction is to rub his leg. I don't know if I'm just emotional or if I'm really just horny, but no matter what the reason is, I'm aroused. Every time Sage rubs my arm and every time I rub his leg, I get wetter.

Sage verbalizes, "You seem to be calm now. We should get back on the road. We have to handle our business. Additionally, I have to see a lot of family. It's been a long time since I've been to Linden."

Sage is right on two fronts. I am calm now and we need to get back on the road. I'm eager to see my boys and don't want to delay that another moment. I sit up and give Sage a hug and thank him for calming me down. I bury my head on his firm chest and he engulfs my upper body in his ripped and solid arms.

Sage is a very handsome man standing just over six feet tall. He's in his late twenties, but doesn't look a day over 22. His hair is silky black and is extremely wavy to the point where someone might think he has a curl. He has a thick mustache and goatee that is well manicured. His sharply cut caramel complexioned face and dreamy light brown eyes have a way of driving women crazy. He has broad shoulders that always look like he's wearing shoulder pads. No matter how big his shirt is it always looks like he's carrying mini bowling balls on his chest.

I feel safe and comforted like this is where I'm meant to be. Sage places a gentle kiss on my collar bone. Why did he do that? He knows my body too well for that to be an accident. The kiss on the collar bone has always been something that turned me on and now is no different. A sharp horniness is poking at me.

While he kisses my collar bone, I smell his mint scented breath. I feel his breath on my neck and its sensation is a turn on. It makes me twitch because it feels so good. I hope he didn't notice because he may take advantage of me in my weak moment.

Sage notices because he kisses my collar bone again and puts a little tongue with it. I should know better than to think anything would get past Sage. I receive the second kiss to my collar bone very well. What a pleasant way to end a much needed talk. Sage always delivers the proper sentiment for the occasion. Just as I think he's only going in for another kiss on my collar bone, he surprises me again. He grabs me by the small of my back and gives me a peck on my lips. I kiss him back as my hands surf his wavy black hair.

The way Sage touches me makes me forget where we are. It's broad daylight and we are at a rest stop making out in the car. I don't care because my body needs this release that I'm sure Sage will provide. He grabs my breasts forcefully. While we kiss, Sage takes one of his hands and pulls my shirt down from my collar. He then proceeds to yank my titty out of my brassiere and with intent begins to suck and nibble on my nipple. My pussy is becoming flooded with my juices. I grab the back of Sage's head and massage it subtly.

It feels like his hands and lips were made solely to surf my body. Sage makes me feel like no other. It still amazes me how after all of this time, Sage still floats my boat. I think loving him so much is the reason why his touch feels so good. My feelings for him are far greater than physical. I love his mind, his humor, and his dick.

"You wanna feel my dick again? You wanna see how hard he is for you?" Sage asks.

"Yes, I do, but this isn't right. There's too much going on between and around us to do this. It'll only complicate things even more. The club, the boys, and Eric and Kevin are just too much to deal with," I say.

"Well, you'll only have to worry about me and the boys very soon. The paternity test will prove that the boys are mine. Besides, we're here now. It's just you and me in this car," Sage vocalizes.

"You're assuming things that are not necessarily fact. We'll see about the test results when they come back," I reply.

"You've said you want it, so stop thinking so much and live in the moment. Live for what we had and what we can be going forward," Sage dictates.

Sage starts kissing me and working my breast again. He knows all of my spots. He spent years learning and surveying my body. I reach along the side of my seat and hit the button to let the seat back. The seat is as flat as can be and Sage is on top of me. He's now switching between licking one breast and fondling the other to licking my neck. I'm overtaken by passion and have no choice but to reach for his dick. Fortunately, the windows have fogged up and nobody can see inside.

The bulge I feel in his pants is rock solid. I want to feel his dick slide inside of me. Sage reaches under me and attempts to pull my sweatpants down, but he's unable to do so because my ass is too juicy to easily pull my pants over it. Without a second's hesitation, I lift my lower body, so Sage can continue his mission.

I'm eager to feel Sage inside of me again. It's been a long time since we've had meaningful sex. The quickie we had last time really doesn't count. The spontaneity of this episode is thrilling in itself. Sage pulls one leg out of my pants and underwear. Now my pussy is fully exposed, but only for a split second. He buries his face in my cunt like he has done masterfully so many times.

When I feel the heat and softness of his tongue on my clit, I sigh in ecstasy. I reach down and pull my lips apart. Now Sage has unimpeded access to my clit. I moan as his tongue licks my clit and enters my pussy. Sage slurps my punani as I become wetter and wetter. It feels so good that I raise my body off of the seat and arch my back while I grab the head rest. Sage moves his tongue faster and faster as I moan and squirm.

"You're a big girl, so stop running from it. I want you to stop running from it and fuck my face," Sage says as he wipes my juices from his face.

I give him what he asks for. I push his head back down into my pussy and lock my legs around his head. Now he can't run and neither can I. Sage eats my pussy like a stallion. He's licking circles on my clit and pussy like a hula hoop circles someone's waist. He begins to penetrate my pussy with his tongue again. I can't take it anymore because his tongue is teasing me. I need to feel his dick inside of me now.

I open my legs and say, "I wanna feel your dick. Put it in me now."

Even after I tell Sage to put his dick in me, he continues to eat me out. I think he wants me to beg for it. I'm so ready to feel it that I grab his head and push it away from my pussy.

"Give it to me now. I miss him inside of me. Stop teasing me and put him in!" I order.

Sage finally makes a move to pull down his pants. The veins in his dick look like lines on a road map. They're everywhere and his brown dick is pulsating from being so hard. He can't lie and say he doesn't want to feel my walls suffocating his rod. He takes his dick and sensually rubs it up, down, and around my pussy area without sticking it in. Why does Sage continue to tease me? I reach down and grab his dick and try to angle it just right for me to slide on his dick, but my attempt fails.

"You seem like you really want it. Do you want it now?" Sage asks.

"Can't you tell by how wet my pussy is that I want it? Did I not tell you I want it?" I ask.

As I lie back in the car seat, I spread my legs wide open for Sage to enter my sweetness. Ideally, I wouldn't want our first time after all of this time to be in the car, but I guess this is what being caught in the moment is all about. I stroke Sage's dick several times and massage the head of his dick too. Sage is ready to fuck me to the point that he has pre-cum on his dick.

"It looks like I'm not the only one who's ready to fuck," I observe.

"No, not at all. I want to just as bad, if not more than you want to. I've been envisioning this day for quite some time now," Sage comments.

Sage goes to insert himself into my pussy, but I stop him. I tell him that I want to have sex with him badly, but in the car may not be the best time. He assures me that having sex in the car is a good idea and we should make it happen. I close my legs and let him know that our time will come, but I don't want to spoil our sexual reunion in the car. He takes my decision pleasantly and does not give me any grief. I'm happy knowing that he wants me just as much as I want him. It would have been nice to feel his head inside of me, but I'll wait and make him earn it.

"You're not mad are you?" I ask.

"Yes, I'm a little mad at myself for not putting it in when you initially told me to. I'm okay other than that," Sage voices jokingly.

"Yes, you should have. You missed your opportunity. That's what you get for teasing me. We could've been getting it in. Well, they say good things come to those who wait. Maybe you'll be the person who good things come to," I state.

Sage agrees with what I said. I grab some wipes out of my purse and clean myself up. Sage gets back in his seat, but never puts his dick back in his pants.

"Sage, are you gonna put him away?" I question.

"Yeah, but I was hoping you'd give me some oral in return and put him to sleep for me. I don't want to ride to Jersey with blue balls," Sage remarks. "It seems like I always end up eating your pussy and never get to make love to you or even get a nut."

I say, "Uh, no! You had your chance to get off and you blew it. It's not my fault that you were playing hard to get. Now you're just hard."

I don't know why he thinks I would give him head right here and now like I'm some type of rest stop hoe. He'll just have to ride with blue balls for the time being. Besides, his dick will go limp eventually. It's not like he'll die on the way to Jersey from having a hard dick. Even though, he might be very uncomfortable.

"I understand. I'll be okay. You're right, it's my fault," Sage acknowledges.

Sage's dick eventually goes soft and we get back on the road. We enjoy hours of stimulating conversation the entire way to Jersey.

Sage and I arrive in New Jersey and he drives to his brother's house where he's going to stay.

"So, what time do you want to link up tomorrow to go to the clinic?" I inquire.

Sage verbalizes, "It doesn't matter to me. This is the only reason I'm here, so you let me know."

"Okay, let's get to the clinic as early as possible. The clinic opens at 8 a.m. sharp and that's also our appointment time, so we should be there as soon as they open," I convey.

Sage replies, "Sounds like a plan to me."

I state, "I'll be here at seven thirty to pick you up."

"I'll be ready at seven, so feel free to come earlier if you want. I would love to spend a few minutes with my sons," Sage asserts.

I utter, "Don't jump the gun with your father and son moments. We haven't proven you to be anything more than a scam artist."

"Ouch, that hurt, but birds of a feather flock together. I guess that's why we are here together now," Sage shoots back.

"Bye Sage. Get out of my car," I say as I chuckle and pop the trunk so he can grab his bag.

After I leave Sage, I drive straight to my mom's house. I can't wait to see my babies. It feels like I haven't seen them in forever. I pull up to my mother's house and dart inside. My boys are in my childhood bedroom resting comfortably. I place a warm kiss on their cheeks and don't disturb them.

My mother and I converse back and forth about the boys and how good they've been. I know they were well behaved because they are angels. I swear I can see a halo over their heads. My mom tells me the particulars of the Disney trip.

We share many stories about motherhood. I also tell her that Sage drove to town with me. She isn't happy about me being with Sage.

"Now, you know I don't get in your business, but I will say this. You really shouldn't have a bunch of men around the boys like that. It's just not healthy," my mom vocalizes.

"Mom, I know that. I wouldn't expose my kids to random men. You taught me better than that," I reply.

My mom communicates, "Okay. I just needed to say it. It's my motherly instinct. You'll find that no matter how old your kids get that you'll always parent them."

"I see that because you're always parenting me," I comment jokingly.

"I'm guilty of being a caring mom. I'm fine with that. You'll always be my baby. With that being said, tell me about why you're with Sage," my mom voices.

"I'm glad you asked. I won't beat around the bush because I know you don't like that. There's a possibility that Sage may be the boys' father," I inform with an embarrassed look on my face.

"Don't give me that look. Own your decisions. I didn't judge you when you told me Kevin and Eric were the boys' fathers and I won't judge you now, but don't ever show weakness or embarrassment," my mom orders sternly.

I should have known she'd respond like that. My mom is one tough cookie. I never met a stronger woman before. Hell, most men aren't as strong as she is. She's always been a fighter.

"I'm owning it Mom. I'm not hiding and I'll accept what the outcome is," I remark.

"You better. I'm not surprised that Sage is still in the picture. You were always sweet on him. I've never known any man to affect you the way he did. I'll say this and then I'm done with this issue. Make sure you get the paternity of the boys determined before they are old enough to know what's going on," dictates Mom.

"I'm way ahead of you. That's why I'm here. That's why he's here. We're taking a paternity test first thing in the morning," I speak.

"That's good to know. The kids deserve better, so be better Sheena," Mom says.

I reply, "I'll be better Mom. I promise."

The truth of the matter is that she's right and I know it. I've been doing some very questionable things lately and it's time I get things back in order. This paternity test will bring much needed closure to a very tumultuous time. I'm looking forward to the end of this chaos. Once it's over, I'll live closer to the teachings of my mother.

I visit Aunt Virginia, a couple of my friends, and other family members with the boys and then return to my mother's house. I wash my babies, feed them, and put them to bed. I kick back and watch a little television. I have to be up early tomorrow, so no need to stay out late. Besides, my boys don't need to be out late anyway. Not to mention that my mother needs a break from caring for them. Hell, I'm tired anyway. I can't hang like I used to. I prepare for bed and fall asleep in my childhood bedroom.

The next morning I wake up to the sound of my boys playing with one another. I love the baby sounds they make. They are the gems of my life. I don't interrupt their brotherly bonding. Instead, I go grab my phone and record this very precious moment. They're absolutely adorable. I can't wait to play this recording for them when they get older.

Okay boys, playtime is over. We have some very serious business to tend to. I'm sorry that I'm putting you two through this, but today marks the end of the drama and a start to a new beginning. I clean the boys up and fix their bottles. My mom watches the boys while I jump in the shower.

After I get dressed, I load the boys up and swing by to pick Sage up. He's ready when we arrive and we drive to the clinic. I never told him which clinic we were going to because I didn't want him to be able to falsify the results of the test as he claims he did the first time around.

We arrive at the clinic promptly at 8 a.m. We walk in and fill out some paperwork. By the time we sit down, we are called to the back for the DNA test to be administered. We're in and out of the clinic before we know it. They inform us that the results will be back in two business days. I'm glad the results will be back so soon.

I really wish I could have the results back sooner, but I will be patient. Sage is really fascinated with the boys. He's more focused on them than me. He must really think that he's their father. I don't know what to think. I just need those results back as soon as possible.

We all go to IHOP for breakfast. After breakfast, I drop Sage off at his friend's house and I run my second errand. I don't trust Sage enough to not think he would manipulate this test too. For that reason, I have another test scheduled at a different clinic. He has no idea about this one or where it is.

I kept the straw from the cup he was drinking from while we were driving up here yesterday, so I have his DNA sample secured. If these tests don't reveal the same information, I'll know Sage is full of shit. The boys and I drive to the second clinic and repeat the same actions from the earlier clinic visit. We leave there and spend the rest of our time visiting family. Sunday morning arrives and it's time to head back to D.C. I pick Sage up and we head for I-95.

The ride is short and sweet. We arrive back in our nation's capital around noon. Sage wants to play with the boys, but I cut that short. There's no need to put the cart before the horse. He'll have plenty of time to play with the boys if he's their father. I think it's better to wait for the results.

CHAPTER 7
Kevin's Perspective

I can't believe Sage pulled a gun on us. I'm even more upset that he had the audacity to shoot at us. He doesn't know who I am. He didn't fight his battle like a man. Instead, he took the cowardly route and used a weapon. If that's the way he wants to play, I'm all for it. I'll meet him at the level of force he exerted and raise him one. He obviously doesn't know the rule of the streets. If you are going to pull a gun, you better use it. Firing a warning shot is basically like not using the gun.

"Are you alright, man? That got a little crazy, didn't it?" I inquire.

"Yeah, I'm cool. A little shook up, but otherwise I'm fine. Never been shot at before. I've had many 'firsts' since I started dealing with Sheena," Eric reports.

"I know what you mean. The idea of getting shot kinda scared me a little bit too. I've seen it in the movies a thousand times and thought nothing of it, but the real thing is terrifying. Sheena has me, well us, doing a bunch of stuff we never expected we'd do," I comment.

"I don't know how I ended up here, but it's getting crazier and crazier by the day," Eric remarks.

"Definitely. You should meet me at the Breakfast Nook. We'll grab a bite and talk things over. Seems like we may have more in common than just Sheena," I say jokingly.

Eric accepts my invitation. We drive our respective cars and meet at the eatery. The place is not packed, so we are quickly seated. The waitress asks us what we want and we order. Eric and I converse.

"I know we met under some very unusual and chaotic circumstances, but I don't think we need to be enemies. We're really only enemies because of the way we were brought together," Eric states.

I reply, "I was thinking the same thing. That's why I extended the breakfast invitation to you. I'm hoping you and I can bury the hatchet today."

"I'm cool with that. It seems we have a common enemy now. Depending on how you look at it, we could possibly have two foes," says Eric.

"Right, Sheena and Sage. They seem to be pretty damn tight now. I don't get how because they've been enemies for a while now. I don't get what's different between now and then," I orate.

"I stopped by Sheena's house the night In the Mix caught fire and she made it seem like she was just helping him with the fire, so maybe that's why," Eric offers.

I comment, "That's bullshit. It had nothing to do with helping him through a troubling situation. Sage was at the house hours before the lounge burned down."

"Really? How do you know that? What's going on?" Eric asks.

"Listen, you have to promise not to tell anyone what I'm about to share with you," I verbalize.

"You have my word on the eyes of my son that I won't break our trust and tell others what you tell me today," Eric asserts.

I lean in towards Eric and in a low voice I narrate, "Alright, so you know the lounge burned down. It was definitely no accident. Sheena came up with an elaborate plan for me to torch the lounge and I carried it out to perfection."

"You have to be shitting me! I don't get what she benefits from having you blaze the spot," Eric states.

I pronounce, "Keep your voice down. You're gonna tell the whole damn world. Here's why. I had sex with Ilesha the night of the

Halloween party, or so I thought, but it turned out that Sage set up a stunt to make me think that. Sheena got wind of the plot and sought revenge on Sage and that's how the lounge got burned down. I poured gasoline all around it and set it ablaze."

"I'm floored. I missed all of that. Now, I see why Sheena was avoiding all of my calls. She was busy plotting and scheming. You know how she is about her girls, she'd burn down all of D.C. for them," Eric mentions.

"I wasn't surprised by how far she was willing to take her revenge because she holds them in such high regard, but what's confusing to me is why she's now riding to New Jersey with Sage," I voice.

"I agree. She said it's business, but you know she's conniving, so you really can't believe much of what she says. I don't know what to think about that," Eric speaks.

"I really don't give two fucks about Sheena at this point in my life. The only important factor in all of this is my son. I'm not playing games when it comes to him. I'll hurt someone behind my son," I say.

Eric chimes in, "I don't blame you for that because I'll hurt someone over my son too! I really don't like how she kept our sons away from us for all of this time."

"Yeah, I don't like this shit either. It's almost like she thinks she's running the show. It's time for us to take control of this situation," I declare.

We talk more about the situation and other things. We realize that we know some of the same people. I learn that the party I went to with my cousin was in fact a birthday party for Eric at the Diamond Center and Sheena was there. We leave breakfast with a new found respect for one another. We also realize that we don't care for Sheena as much as we once did. Her distrustful ways have made us this way. I find it hard to believe that I don't care for Sheena the way I once did, but it has happened. I never thought that I could stop loving her. I'm almost to the point where I don't like seeing her face at all.

People often talk about a woman scorned, but skip over a man being scorned. Well, Eric and I are exactly that. I'm tired of being lied to and treated as if I'm less than a person. She can have Sage or whoever she wants because I'm finished with her. In fact, I think I may need to consider trying to get joint custody of my son. The courts will at least grant me that. I may even be able to get full custody of Devin if the courts become aware of Sheena's scandalous ways. Hmmm, I may have to drop a dime on her if need be. I know they'll question her integrity when I tell them that she has twins by two different men.

My phone is ringing. Who's calling me this early in the morning? It's probably Sheena calling to complain about what happened to Sage. I hope she doesn't expect me to apologize or be sympathetic because I'm not. We gave Sage every opportunity to not get in Sheena's car, but he refused to listen, so he had to get pummeled. I finally pull my phone out of my pocket and look at the screen. I don't recognize the number with certainty, but it does look familiar. I decide to answer the call anyway.

"Hello," I say hesitantly.

"Hi, how are you?" asks a female.

I inquire immediately, "Who is this?"

"Oh, that's how you're gonna do me? You don't remember the night of passion we spent together on Halloween after the party?" she asks.

"Wow! I never thought I'd hear from you again. I deleted your number after that long text you sent me. I figured it was a one night thing between us. Shit, I thought you were someone else altogether," I respond.

"Yes, I know. I thought it would be a one night stand and I had no intention of contacting you again even though I enjoyed the night thoroughly. Besides, I heard that we were both misled that night. I got my ass beat for us having sex," she states.

"Mislead is quite an understatement, don't you think? Who beat your ass? By the way, what's your name? Sage didn't hit you did he?" I interrogate.

"My name is Leslie and no, Sage didn't hit me, but your girlfriend and some other girl she was with did. Apparently, I was impersonating one of them. It was a huge scene in the bathroom. I'm sorry about what happened to you in the club. I was there when you and Sage fought," verbalizes Leslie.

"Damn, I had no idea they attacked you. I'm truly sorry. It was probably my ex-girlfriend Sheena and her best friend Ilesha who assaulted you. Yeah, that fight with Sage was nothing. I had a few drinks that day and he took advantage of my weakened state. I wasn't at my best," I reply.

"I understand. Well, I just called to apologize and check on you. I hope I didn't cause you too much harm just because I wanted to fuck you," Leslie remarks.

"No harm here. I thoroughly enjoyed the night and it's what I wanted to do, so you don't need to say sorry. I just wish we could link back up and maybe spend some more time together. I'm not the least bit upset with you," I voice.

"Kevin, I like the sound of that, but I'm slightly embarrassed that we had sex on the first night without even knowing each other. I hope you don't think I'm a hoe," Leslie speaks.

I shoot back, "I'm in no position to judge you. I have my own set of questionable decisions, so it's all good with me. I don't think you're a hoe."

"Well, that's good to know. You were amazing in bed that night and I would like a few more sex sessions with you. I'll be honest with you, half of me wants to fuck you again to spite your ex and the other half of me thinks you're special. Nobody has ever made my body feel the way you did that night," Leslie reports.

"I love your honesty. Well, I definitely want to see you again. It's funny because I think the night we shared was awesome too. We can build on that. We can be open and honest with the things we do. No pressure," I orate.

"Okay, that sounds real nice. Well, save my number and give me a call. I'm not working right now because somebody burned the lounge down, so I'll be free for the most part. All I have is school," Leslie conveys.

"I'll save your number as soon as we hang up. We'll hang out soon. I know it's crazy the way we met, but I'm glad we did. Talk to you soon," I say.

Leslie and I end the call. I'm glad I answered the call because I could have missed out on Leslie. This is proof that there are plenty of fish in the sea. I'm right back in action. She'll be screaming my name very soon. I don't know what Eric's going to do because he's not going to be able to snap back as quickly as me. He doesn't have any women on his roster. Maybe Leslie will have some friends that he can hook up with in the future. It's funny how Eric and I were both just enemies and now we're on the same team.

CHAPTER 8
Sheena's Perspective

It's Monday morning and time to start the day. First, I get my sons cleaned up and fed, and then I get myself together. I have to drop them off at daycare myself, since Eric and Kevin are mad at me. I'm sure one of them would be okay with dropping the boys off, but I want to limit their access to the boys for the next couple of days until the results come back. I don't mind the little bit of extra running I'll have to do. It allows me to spend a little more time with the boys and I'm all for that. I have everything secured and I'm ready to leave the house when the doorbell rings.

I'm not expecting anyone, so the doorbell ringing is totally a surprise. I look out the window and see Eric's car outside. I open the door to see what he wants. Eric is standing there in his work suit looking quite dapper. He probably went overboard for me, but I don't care.

I inquire, "What are you doing here?"

"Umm, what kind of question is that? You know what day it is?" Eric asks.

"Right, it's your day to take the boys to daycare. I totally dismissed that. With all that's happened, I didn't think you'd be willing to take them," I comment.

Eric asserts, "Nothing will keep me from my fatherly duties. I know things are awry between us, but that doesn't impact the boys one bit. We are grownups, so we have to make sure what we have going on doesn't hurt the boys."

"I understand and whole-heartedly agree, but I think I'll take the boys today. I already had it in my mind to do so anyway," I pronounce.

"No, no, I'm here now and I haven't seen Deric in far too long, so I'll take them. It's on the way to the school anyway. Much easier for me to take them," Eric offers.

I think it's in my best interest to not argue with Eric on this one. I'll allow him to take them, but tomorrow is a different story. I don't want to start the day off on the wrong foot. I acquiesce and go get the boys' belongings for Eric. Eric attempts to walk inside my house to help with their stuff, but I stop him.

"Eric, you can just wait outside the door. You don't have the privilege of being inside of my house. Those privileges have been revoked," I dictate.

"Sheena, I am here for the boys. I really don't have much to say to you. Stop being petty and let me do my fatherly duties. I don't care about stepping foot in your house. I have a lot of things on my mind and the last thing you want is for me to unload them on you right now," Eric speaks.

"I don't want to hear them, so please keep them to yourself. One thing I will say to you is don't ever stop by here unexpectedly again. You don't have that privilege anymore either. I'm not playing with you," I order.

"What a bitch? Can't be civil to save your damn life. You could have told us the boys would be back in town yesterday, but you're a selfish bitch," Eric charges.

I slam the door in Eric's face and lock it. I'll just do what I planned to do before he arrived. I go to the garage and put the boys and our things in the car. I jump in the car and back out. Hopefully, Eric won't stand in the way and block me from getting out of the garage. I may have to just run his ass over. Unfortunately, he does block my path. I stop the car and roll down the window.

I vocalize calmly, "You'll get one warning to move and then I'll hit the gas and if you get hit you just get hit. The choice is yours."

Eric takes my warning for a joke and does not move. He's about five feet behind my car blocking my path. I stick to my guns and step on the gas. The car goes in reverse after letting out a loud screech. Eric dives out of the way of the car just before he gets hit. I hit the garage door button and proceed to taking my boys to daycare.

I loathe starting the day off with negative energy because it seems to set the tone for the rest of the day. I'll do my best to not let Eric's nonsense influence me. I have a meeting with two potential clients at 9 o'clock sharp and the last thing I need is for them to sense negativity from me. If the meeting doesn't go smoothly, it could be the determining factor in my company acquiring them.

After I drop the boys off, I head to the office. While I'm driving, I get a call from Kevin. I know better than to answer his call. I'm sure it'll be a call filled with anger and frustration. My nerves have calmed down from the fiasco with Eric and there is no need to get my blood boiling again. I play it smart and send Kevin to voicemail. If he leaves a message, I'll check it later. I don't even want to chance his message making me upset.

I make it to the office and prepare for my 9 o'clock. While I'm prepping, Kevin sends me a text message. Unfortunately, I couldn't avoid reading what he sent. He wants me to call him now because he has some stuff on his mind that he feels we need to discuss. I inform him via text that I'll call him once I'm free at work. It's evident he wants to argue because he replies back with an insolent text about not letting him know the boys and I were back in town.

I don't respond to the text and instead turn my phone off. I need my head to be clear for my meeting. In fact, I'll call him when my work day is complete. I'm definitely not on his or Eric's timetable. It's all about me and my boys. I have to admit that I'm extremely anxious to get these DNA test results back.

My 9 o'clock is here and the meeting is going as planned. The potential client seems to like what I'm presenting and it's looking real good for me to land this new acquisition. This is how I like to start my work week. By the end of the meeting, the potential client has become a new account. The contracts have been signed and I'm happy to bring them onboard. The rest of the day is business as usual. I have no other pressing affairs to attend to.

I order lunch for my employees as a token of my appreciation for their hard work and to celebrate us acquiring a new client. The day started off shaky, but certainly turned in the right direction. I leave the office shortly after my employees and I finish eating lunch. I want to get my boys early to spend some time with them. I missed them while they were gone, so I want to try to get some of the time I missed back. I drive to the daycare to pick them up.

"I'm here to pick up Devin and Deric Mills," I

say to an employee at the daycare facility.

She responds, "I'll go get them."

The woman is taking longer than normal to return and I grow impatient. I decide to walk to the back to see what the delay is. As I'm walking to the back, the attendant who I initially spoke with is walking back to the front. Unfortunately, she does not have my boys with her and I immediately grow concerned.

"Ma'am, I'm confused. You don't have my sons with you," I mention.

"I went in the back to get them, but it appears that your sons have been picked up already," she informs.

My body is overtaken with fear, worry, and rage all in one instance. I don't know what I'll do if something happens to my boys.

"What the hell you mean they've been picked up? Who the hell did you give my babies to?" I angrily ask.

"Ms. Mills, I need you to calm down and not use that tone of voice with me. The sign out log shows that your sons were picked up by Eric Burns. He is listed as a parent and is authorized to pick the boys up," she states.

My attitude towards her is adjusted once she tells me that. I know the boys are fine and that they will be well taken care of. I'm still mad that Eric didn't tell me that he was going to pick them up. I will deal with him as soon as I see him.

I voice, "I'm sorry for getting loud with you.

Eric didn't tell me that he was picking the boys up today. I was just nervous at first. I do apologize."

"No need to apologize because I have children too, so I know how you feel. I'd also flip out if something happened to them," the attendant responds.

I say, "Thanks for understanding."

I leave the daycare and call Eric as soon as I step foot out the door. He can't possibly think what he did was right. Eric could have sent me a text to inform me that he was going to pick them up. That few breaths of worry seemed like an eternity. I'm giving him an ear full for sure.

"Are you out of your damn mind? Where are my sons?" I inquire.

"Well, hello to you too. You seem to be upset for some unknown reason to me. You should calm your nerves, Sheena," Eric says sarcastically.

"Don't play with me Eric. You know I'm not the one to play with. Again, the boys," I demand.

"You seem to not know that you aren't the only parent here. I picked the boys up because you are holding them hostage from us. I had to do what I had to do," Eric explains.

"You could have sent a text or called me to let me know. I drove there for nothing and almost cursed the staff out because of you. Well, I'm coming to pick them up from you," I inform.

"I don't need to tell you when I'm gonna pick my son up. I did what I wanted to do just like you do. You want us to keep your feelings in mind, but you don't do the same thing for us. This is fair. I'm at the mall with Deric and I dropped Devin with Kevin. I have no idea where they are. We're not finished having our father son time, so you won't be picking Deric up from me," Eric reports.

I'm livid, but I decide to be the bigger person right now. I don't feel like arguing anymore. I'll let them enjoy their time with the boys. For all I know, this could be their last time with the boys. Where are those test results? I don't want Eric or Kevin to know my thoughts about them picking the boys up anyway. It was obviously done to spite me.

I vocalize, "Okay, I understand. Enjoy the time with your son. I will be home, so just let me know when you're on your way to drop Deric off."

Eric lets me know that he'll bring Deric back later. I text Kevin to tell him to inform me when he's on his way back with Devin. He agrees to what I asked. I call my girls to vent. Hopefully, they are free to chat. Unfortunately, neither one of them answers. Ilesha is probably live on air at the radio station and Rachel is probably firing somebody. It's cool because this isn't a real emergency, but they'll be interested to know what happened anyway. They like to be in the loop of everything that affects me and their godchildren.

I decide to have a few hours of "me time".

There's no reason not to take advantage of this unexpected free time. I drive to the salon to get my nails and eyebrows done. After I get those things done, I stop by the massage parlor. I leave the massage parlor and head to the liquor store. A couple of drinks once I get home will top my outing off with a cherry, literally.

I make it home and enjoy a couple of amaretto sours with heavy cherries. These drinks are heaven as they hit my palate. The only thing that would make this moment better is if my girls were here. I text my girls a picture of the drinks they're missing out on. Ilesha responds with a picture of her own. She sends me a picture of a huge bottle of vodka that she and her boyfriend are sipping on. I can only imagine the kinky things that are going on over there.

A moment later, Rachel texts me. She was at the movies with her man. She is desirous of my drink, but is not going to make it over. She has some adult activities to partake in with her man. It's still unbelievable that I lost both of my men and a convenient situation with them. Oh well, by myself it is. I've been here before.

I know Eric and Kevin need to bring my boys back soon. I hope they'll be somewhat respectful and bring them back at a decent hour. You know what? I'll call them to tell them what time to bring my boys back. I dial Eric first and get no response. Unfortunately, I call Kevin and get no response from him either. Now, this is the shit I don't like.

They know I have to work tomorrow and they're being very inconsiderate. I'm going to give them an earful when I touch bases with them. They've taken my kindness for weakness and I have to set things straight. Another hour has passed and still no word from Kevin or Eric. I'm on the verge of calling the cops or going to their homes to retrieve my most valued possessions. Just as I get dressed, my phone begins to ring. Kevin is calling, so I answer the phone.

"Well, hello. I've been looking for you for a long damn time. I really don't like this bullshit stunt you and Eric pulled today," I exclaim.

"We didn't pull any stunt. We are simply two men who wanted to see their children and we did just that. I never thought you'd be the woman to keep her kids from their father. Hell, there are many things I thought you wouldn't do, so I don't know why I'm shocked now," Kevin states.

I voice, "I never kept you from them. You two need to understand that there's a lot going on and I'm trying to put things in order. We'll settle that soon, but for now, you need to bring Devin home. It's late and I need to get him and myself ready for tomorrow."

Kevin responds, "That's why I'm calling. I wanted to tell you that we are keeping the boys tonight. I have Devin with me and Eric has Deric with him. We'll be certain to take good care of them tonight and get them dropped off tomorrow."

"Excuse me, but you and your boyfriend don't decide where my sons go if I don't approve of it. You and Eric need to bring the boys home tonight or you'll have hell to pay," I dictate.

"Sheena, I think you seem to forget that these are our children too. You aren't running a dictatorship here. Eric didn't want to call or text you that we were keeping them, but I thought better of it. I didn't want you to call the cops or something ridiculous," Kevin explains.

"When it comes to my boys, it is definitely a dictatorship. Fuck you and Eric. You two wanna indulge in juvenile games I see. Well, I don't have time for this. Enjoy your time with the boys because this may be your last night with them," I say.

Kevin replies, "I can promise you one thing and it's that I'll definitely be seeing my son after tonight and tomorrow. If I have to go to the courts to get it done, I will."

I hang up on Kevin because I really don't feel like hearing him go on any further. The truth is that it's late and there's no reason to argue with a fool. I'll get my boys tomorrow and go from there. I don't need this stress in my life. I jump in the shower and call it a night afterwards.

CHAPTER 9
Sheena's Perspective

It's time to start another day. I'm afraid to see what this day has in store for me. I'm afraid because I'm hoping that I don't have to seriously injure Kevin and Eric if they don't bring my boys home today. I'm apprehensive about the results of the paternity test with Sage. I don't know what to think about Sage being truthful or not. Either way, I'll find out today when those results come back. There's a lot riding on these test results. This will obviously impact my twins for the rest of their lives. Additionally, Kevin and Eric will be livid if they aren't the fathers. I'll be impacted too, but probably the least out of all parties involved. Sage will have two children who he'll be responsible for.

I have a tremendous burden to carry, but I'm equipped to make it through. I get myself together for the day ahead and go to my office. My employees greet me and come back to my office for a brief meeting. I just want everyone to be on the same page for today's happenings just in case I have to step out to handle my personal business. After the meeting, my employees go back to their duties. I call the daycare that my boys attend to see if they've been dropped off. I hate that I have to call the daycare to find out, but with the arguing I've been doing with Eric and Kevin this seems to be the simplest way to avoid conflict.

"Wee Care Daycare, how can I help you?" asks the daycare employee.

"Hi, my name is Sheena Mills. I'm the mother of Deric and Devin Mills and I want to know if they've been dropped off today," I say.

She replies, "I'll find out for you. Hold for one moment please."

The lady comes back to the line and informs me that Deric and Devin have both been dropped off. I'm glad they're there because I really don't want to have to play another game of find the missing twins. I should go to the daycare and pick them up early. That way I won't have to worry about Eric and Kevin picking them up again today.

I put out a couple fires at work and decide to go get my boys while I'm on lunch break. I pick them up, grab my lunch, and head back to my office. It's taking me forever and a day to get to my office to eat because all the girls in the office are going crazy over my munchkins. I understand they haven't seen them in a while, but the way they're carrying on you'd think they were celebrities. I finally get to my office and close the door. While I'm eating my salad, I receive a phone call from a New Jersey area code. I hope this is the call I've been waiting for since Saturday.

"Hello," I answer.

"This is Carlton from New Jersey Lab Corp. I'm calling for Ms. Mills," he says.

I state, "Hi, Carlton. This is Ms. Mills."

"Ms. Mills, I'm calling to inform you of the results of a recent paternity test your children took this past Saturday," Carlton says.

"Yes, I've been waiting for your call," I speak.

"Before I proceed, I just need you to confirm some information, so I can verify that this is in fact Ms. Mills," Carlton says.

Carlton asks me a series of questions about my account. Doesn't he know that I'm ten years beyond eager to find out the test results? He's making me wait and it's driving me crazy. I know he has to follow protocol, but damn, just tell me the information already. Finally, after several questions Carlton is done. Now, he's ready to reveal the results of the DNA test.

"We've run our tests and it shows that Sage McMillan is the father of both Devin and Deric Mills. The test reveals that the percentage of Sage

McMillan being the father is 99.9 percent," Carlton reports.

"Thank you, so much. I appreciate your time and thanks for calling. Oh, one more thing. I was told that I would be emailed the results and mailed a hard copy," I voice.

Carlton informs, "I'm sending the email now, so you should have that momentarily. As far as the hard copy, it will go out in the mail tomorrow and be to you no later than Monday."

He asks me if I have any more questions and I inform him that I don't have anything else to ask him. I thank Carlton again and end the call. So, Sage is the father according to this clinic. Now, I need to get the results from the other clinic I had perform the DNA tests. If the clinic Sage didn't know about reports the same thing, it's certified. Deep down inside I want Sage to be the father. I'd rather my boys have the same father than to have two different ones. On the flip side, I'm sure Eric and Kevin will lose their minds if these results are confirmed by the other facility. What is a woman to do? Well, I can't worry about Kevin and Eric at this point. I have my babies to consider. Besides, what's done is done.

I go on with the rest of my work day. I work while I keep my boys comfortable. The rest of the day is uneventful. I pack up my work items, shut down my computer, and take my boys to the car. I get home, change the boys, and fix myself something to eat. I text Rachel and Ilesha to see if they're available to stop by. I tell them that the boys miss them, but I also miss them. I really need to tell them everything that's going on. Fortunately, they're both available to come over.

My girls make it over about an hour after I initially texted them. It seems like I haven't seen them in an eternity. It really hasn't been that long, but I love their company, so the absence is just exacerbated. Ilesha and Rachel storm in the house like normal and run straight for the boys. They both have teddy bears for them. They pick them up and the boys are all smiles. Hell, Rachel and Ilesha are smiling more than the boys are. I guess I'm the fifth wheel.

"Ladies, I am here too," I say jokingly.

"Girl, we see you. We'll get to you after we give Devin and Deric our kisses. We haven't seen them in forever. We see you all the time," Ilesha utters.

Rachel shares, "She's right. You can be patient. We haven't laid eyes on our godsons in a long time. Don't be selfish my dear."

I take her advice and give them their time. I don't want to infringe on their bonding. I take pictures of them holding the boys and upload them to Instagram. I don't have much else to do right now.

"Well, I'm glad your ass decided to do something productive. After you take a few more pictures, go fix us some drinks. That's what you need to be doing," Ilesha mandates.

I go to the kitchen and fix the girls a drink. I'm not drinking tonight because I had my fix yesterday. I walk back over to the girls with their drinks. They put the boys down and I hand them their drinks.

"Hey, girl. How've you been?" Ilesha asks.

"Now you ask? How long have you two been here now?" I question.

"Darling, it hasn't been that long. You know we are here for you too," Rachel remarks.

"Bitch, you're fine. Your boys are healthy and you're healthy. Ain't nothing wrong with you, so don't think you're getting any sympathy from me. Tell us what's going on," Ilesha verbalizes.

"Our ears and shoulders are yours," Rachel asserts.

I tell the girls all about the scuffle and shooting that occurred at my house. Naturally, Ilesha begins her normal man bashing and Rachel just wants an end to the nonsense. I also inform them of the results of the first paternity test Sage took. Rachel and Ilesha both agree that it's in the best interest of the boys for Sage to be the father. They are hoping that the secret DNA tests reveal the same results.

"In a lot of cases two is better than one, but in the case of the boys and their fathers, two is definitely not better than one," says Rachel.

Ilesha chimes in, "I know two is better than one in the case of these drinks. Take your ass in the kitchen and get me another drink," orders

Ilesha. "Girl, that first one was tasty as hell I mean like oh my goodness girl! Hell, if I didn't know any better I'd think some of my pussy was in that drink."

I fix Ilesha another drink and then we brainstorm the best possible ways to tell the guys they aren't the father if that holds true. We discuss why over the phone is better than in person. We also talk about potentially just mailing the results to Kevin's and Eric's houses. It looks like a face to face meeting is the best way to accomplish disseminating the news.

"At this point, we don't know what the truth is, so all we can do is wait," I state.

"Yes, as sneaky as Sage is, we don't know if he found a way to manipulate these test results too," Rachel speaks.

Ilesha asks, "When are you expecting to hear from the other clinic?"

"I was hoping today, but it's getting late, so maybe they'll call me tomorrow," I convey.

"Okay, keep me posted. I'm gonna head home. I have a big day ahead of me tomorrow," Ilesha orates.

"I guess I will head out too, sister," Rachel informs.

The girls depart and I get my boys ready for bed. I check my emails to see what may be ahead for me tomorrow and also to look at the results of the DNA test. To my surprise, there is an email from the second lab in my inbox. I click on the email as if my life depends on it. I scrutinize every inch of the email and finally find the information I seek. This report confirms that Sage is also the father. I'm very happy for the boys because this will make things that much easier for them growing up. I text the girls the great news and they are happy for me. I'll let Sage know tomorrow. I dread telling Eric and Kevin the truth, but it must be done.

Morning is here and I'm upset it arrived so quickly. I really didn't sleep very well, but I'm not surprised. The tossing and turning is due to me worrying about the information I have to share today. I'm worried because I have no idea how this is going to go. Well, I know Sage is going to be excited, so I'm not concerned with that. Unfortunately, I know Kevin and Eric will be devastated to say the least, but I don't know how far their anger will take them.

When the girls and I met last night, we decided that the best way to tell Kevin and Eric the news is to meet them face to face and somewhere public. They will only be able to go to a certain level with their reaction to this heartbreaking information. Can't I just go somewhere and hide from this and wait for things to settle?

I drag myself out of bed and get myself together for the day. I'm not going to the office today, so I email my staff to make them aware of my absence. The boys are going to stay with me today. I have to meet Sage today and I want the boys with me, so I can formally introduce them to their father. I know it's kind of corny, but I think it's necessary. I call Sage.

"Hey, good morning," I say.

"Good morning. It's rather early. I wasn't expecting you to call," Sage speaks.

I reply, "I know it's early, but I was hoping to catch you before you made plans today. I'm hoping we can meet."

"Well, you're in luck today because I'm free. It's not like I have job to go to," Sage sarcastically remarks.

Of course he's talking about not being able to go to the lounge because I orchestrated it being burned down.

I attest, "I'm not sorry about the lounge because you earned that and you know it. Anyway, what time can we meet up?"

"Maybe I did deserve what I got. I can meet at 1 o'clock," Sage says.

I reply, "Okay, sounds good. Let's meet at the sub shop. We can chat there. I have a craving for a turkey and cheese."

"I'll be there," Sage says.

CHAPTER 10
Sheena's Perspective

We hang up and I relax on the couch and play with my boys. I play the scenario of me telling Sage the news over and over. I don't know why I'm trying to predict how this is going to go. It's going to go very smoothly.

It's a quarter before one, so I gather my boys and drive to the sub shop. When we pull up to the shop, Sage is standing out front. He walks over to my car and helps me get the boys out of the car. He better get used to helping with the boys because it's his duty now. We walk inside and get settled in. Sage takes immediately to the boys. He's so into them that he isn't even paying the waiter any attention when he asks us what we want to order.

"Sage," I call. "The waiter is waiting for you to order something."

"Oh, I'm sorry. I just can't get over how perfect they are. I'm at a loss for words. I'll have a turkey and cheese. Light mayo. Nothing else on the sandwich," Sage says.

The waiter writes down the order and walks away.

"Well, I'm glad you're taking such an interest in the boys. I'm sure you can gather why I asked you to meet me today," I voice.

"I'm almost one hundred percent sure that you got the results of the paternity test. If that's the case, you probably want to share the results with me," Sage suggests.

I reply, "You're absolutely correct. The results show that you're the father of Deric and Devin. I have the email they sent me with the results printed out for you to verify. Here you go."

I put the papers in front of Sage, but he doesn't even care to look at them. Instead, he gets out of his seat and picks up Devin. I guess he knew all along what the results would reveal.

"Aren't you going to look at the results?" I ask.

Sage comments, "No, I don't need to look at the results again. I saw the first results that I initially gave you. I know they are my sons and they're perfect. Also, the lab called me yesterday with the results and sent me an email as they did you."

"I see. You could have called me and told me they contacted you. I agree, the boys are perfect," I utter.

"Now, we both know if I would have called you and told you what they told me, you wouldn't have believed me anyway. I figured you'd call when they confirmed what I've known for some time now," Sage conveys.

I laugh to myself because he's right. There is no way in hell I would have believed him. I still have some questions about why he chose to wait to say something. We could have prevented this fiasco with Kevin and Eric from ever happening. I've endured countless days of stress over this situation. I've even interrupted my girls' lives to make things work with Eric and Kevin. Unfortunately, there's more stress to come because Eric and Kevin will not take this news lightly.

"Hell, you're right. I damn sure wouldn't have believed you. Trusting you isn't always the easiest. I have a question that I need answered from you though," I verbalize.

"I don't blame you for questioning my honesty. I'm all ears. Ask me anything," Sage orates.

"Well, you've clearly known for quite some time that you were the boys' father. You could have saved me and those men a lot of trouble by coming forward, but you chose not to. I want to know why you didn't come forward with the paternity test from the very beginning," I voice.

"There are a couple of reasons why I held the information. One was because I was a bit afraid of the idea of being a father. Secondly, I knew you were dating two men and I figured you were head over heels for them. I didn't see room for me in the equation at that time, so I waited. I made my move at the celebration they had when the boys were first born when they initially found out. I thought for sure they would end the relationship with you, but I was wrong," Sage narrates.

"Really, how'd you know what I was up to? Were you telling other people my business?" I inquire.

Sage asserts, "No, I didn't tell anyone. The only person who knew outside of me was my contact at the clinic you went to. I would have come forward after they stayed with you, but I wanted to expose Kevin and Eric for the weaklings they are. Let's be honest. You had to find it strange that they decided to share you versus walking away," Sage speaks.

I remark, "I was wondering how they could be onboard, but I came to the conclusion that they must really love me."

"Now, there may have been some love there, but I doubt it was much. I sent Leslie to sleep with Kevin, so you'd see his true self. I knew Eric would fall off on his own," Sage explains.

"Yeah, both of them really exposed themselves. I didn't see their behavior changing so drastically. They are very vulgar and disrespectful," I admit.

"I see that. They attacked me, so I know they have another side to them. I'm not sorry for exposing them, but I am sorry for putting your friendship with Ilesha in jeopardy. That was a mistake on my part. Again, I apologize," Sage expresses.

"Yes, that was poor judgment on your part. Downright stupid, selfish, and evil. I'm glad it didn't go too far with my girl. That would have been catastrophic. Well, that's behind us now, and we have the boys before us now," I verbalize.

"We sure do and I'm ready to do what's right. I regret displacing my responsibilities on Kevin and Eric. I'll never miss another moment of my sons' lives. I promise you that," Sage narrates.

I say, "I don't need you to promise me that you'll be around. You need to do it. The boys need you to help secure the best lives possible for them."

Sage assures me that he's around for the long haul. He claims that he's done playing games and that the boys are his number one priority. Only time will tell if his words are genuine. He also states that he wants to be there when I tell Eric and Kevin about the new found information.

"Another thing that we need to discuss is the status of In the Mix. You have some damning evidence against me that I burned the lounge down. I won't be able to help the boys financially if I'm out of business," Sage voices.

I reply, "I thought about that last night. I

came to the conclusion that I'll just hold onto the evidence I have against you. You have to support my babies."

"Great, so does that mean I can get my insurance company to take care of things?" Sage asks.

"Yes, my sons need their father to have gainful employment, so you'll need to get the lounge back up and running," I attest.

"You're right. They'll need it for sure. I'll be calling the insurance company very soon," Sage says.

"If it weren't for that, I'd hold this evidence over your head forever. That would be what you deserve," I comment.

We leave the sub shop after eating and conversing. Sage has some calls to make pertaining to getting the lounge taken care of. I'm okay with that because I have some running to do with the boys and I need to call Kevin and Eric to schedule a meeting to tell them what's new.

I'm glad Sage volunteered to be with me when I tell them. I'm sure I'll need him for protection. I was going to have my girls support me again, but I won't be needing them. Hell, Sage may not be enough. I may need a police escort to keep me safe.

I text Eric and Kevin in a group chat and ask them to meet me at Outback Steakhouse. Kevin asks if I'll have the boys with me and if not, he's not coming. I let him and Eric know that the boys will be with me. They both agree to meet me at Outback at six o'clock. Now, I'm nervous. The uncertainty of this meeting has me slightly perspiring. I text Sage to let him know what time and where we're meeting and he agrees to meet us there.

Six o'clock is here and me and the boys are inside the restaurant. Surprisingly, Sage is not here yet. He's always on time if not early. Kevin and Eric are at the bar drinking when I walk in with the boys. I get seated and then text them to come to the table.

They walk over to the table and play with the boys. Their faces are filled with so much glee that I'm tearing up from knowing the heartbreak they're about to experience. I know if someone told me today that my boys weren't mine, I'd die on the spot. I would also want somebody to pay dearly for what they did to me.

"What did you call us here for this time? What's going on in Sheena's world?" asks Kevin.

"Right, I'm sure there's something. We know you didn't call us down here for us to see the boys cause you didn't want us to see them the other day," Eric chimes in.

I reply, "Okay, there is something I want to tell you, but it's not very easy to say."

I'm very reluctant to share the information with them, but I have no choice but to spit it out. Kevin and Eric are both staring at me waiting to see what I need to say. Maybe I'll just hand them copies of the paternity test and let them realize for themselves what's going on.

That's exactly what I'll do. They're going to want to read it anyway, so that's my plan. As I look through my purse for the results, Sage walks up to the table and has a seat. I feel a little more confident about this now.

"What the hell are you doing here? Why didn't you tell us he was coming?" Eric asks.

"You know we don't like you, so I don't see the point of you being here. I guess you two are a couple now," states Kevin. "I should fuck your punk ass up right now."

"I don't care that you don't like me. I'm okay with that. What I'm here to do is support Sheena. She has something to tell you that's very important and so do I," Sage speaks.

"Well, spit it out because we don't have all night to waste," Kevin orders.

I state, "This is hard to say, so bear with me. I know you two have been great fathers to the boys, but…"

Eric cuts me off and states, "Don't tell us that we can't be around the boys anymore. You being with Sage doesn't mean shit to me. I'll be with my son."

"Damn right," says Kevin.

"Fellas, please let her speak. She has to finish what she's trying to tell you two," Sage voices.

"I was going say that a major and inexcusable

error was made in determining paternity of the boys. There was mix-up at the clinic. It appears that you two aren't the boys' fathers," I report.

Their faces are now filled with confusion and anger. I see the blood boiling inside of them. I slide the results to them and they overlook the paper. They are not happy to say the least.

"Here we go again. There's more bullshit in here than at a rodeo. I don't believe this shit. You got us down here to tell us some more garbage. I don't need this paper to tell me who my son is." vocalizes Kevin.

Eric asks, "Why should we believe this paper this time? How do we know this one is real versus the last one?"

"Eric, I don't give a fuck what that paper indicates. I know who my son is and nobody is going to take him from me. Not Sheena, not the damn courts, not a damn soul," Kevin screams.

"Well, that's where you're wrong. Devin isn't your son and Deric isn't your son. As the results of the DNA tests show, I'm their father," Sage reports.

"Oh, hell no! I know you two aren't trying to pull some father switch-a-roo now that you two are back together!" Kevin yells. "I knew I shouldn't have followed you up Sheena."

Eric chimes in, "Sheena, there's no way in hell that you two are gonna tell me that my son, isn't my son. I fell in love with my boy the first time I laid eyes on him. I won't stand for this shit you're trying to pull."

"Guys, I hear what you're saying and I understand why you're upset. I get it. I would be too, but this isn't about us. It's about the boys. If you care for them the way you claim, you will allow the boys to form a relationship with their true father," I articulate.

Kevin and Eric are in total opposition to what we are telling them. Everything they say is loud and filled with vulgarities. We are making a huge scene and garnering a lot of unwanted attention. We are so disruptive that the manager approaches us.

"Hi, I don't want to interrupt, but I'm receiving a lot of complaints about some unruly behavior coming from this party. I'm going to need for it to stop or I will have to ask all of you to leave," states the manager.

I respond, "I apologize for our volume. We'll calm down. Again, I'm sorry."

The manager takes my apology and retreats back to his office. I ask the guys to control themselves because we're upsetting the customers. Sage is calm, but Eric and Kevin are still irate. I don't think there's anything I can do to calm them down.

I speak, "I know this is hard to accept and I'm sure you will want to get your own paternity tests done to ease your mind. Since this is my fault, I will pay for the tests myself."

"Well, fellas it's not totally her fault. I actually

had the initial paternity tests altered to reflect that you two were the fathers. I shouldn't have done that. It was a very immature move on my part and for that, I'm deeply sorry. I was acting immaturely and selfishly," Sage conveys.

"Wait, wait. It makes sense that this is more of your bullshit. I'll definitely be having a test performed. I'm not taking your word for it this time," Eric says.

"I feel badly about this. I know you've spent a lot of time and money with the boys, so I want to pay you back the money you've invested in them to this point. I wish I could also give you your time back, but I can't," Sage remarks.

He pulls out his checkbook and is prepared to write Kevin and Eric a check for the money they've spent on the boys. I think that's a very nice gesture because he doesn't have to offer them anything. Unfortunately, Kevin and Eric aren't flattered by Sage's generosity. Instead, they're quite insulted by it. Eric smacks Sage's checkbook out of his hands to the floor. Sage has a devilish look on his face from Eric's action, but he doesn't react. He picks up the checkbook and puts it in his back pocket.

"You can't turn our heads with your money. We have our own money and definitely don't need yours. Fuck both of you," Kevin says.

"Yeah, I make enough money to not need yours. You can take your money and shove it up your fucking ass," Eric words.

"Guys, you don't need to talk like that. We can keep this peaceful and respectful. We came here to set the record straight, not to be violent and antagonistic," I dictate.

"You come here to tell us that our children aren't ours. I know you couldn't have expected this to be a friendly meeting. Put the shoe on the other foot and think how you'd respond," Eric orates.

"I understand your feelings are hurt, but I won't allow you two to make a big scene in front of my sons. In fact, this will be the last time you see them in a social setting. I know you'll want to have paternity determined, so you have to see them at that point, but after that, it's over. We don't need to confuse the boys any further," Sage utters.

Kevin walks over to Sage and stands toe to toe with him. Neither one of them is backing down. I'm sure this will be a repeat of the fight at In the Mix. I can't allow the boys to see this if it happens. I don't say anything to these grown men acting like barbarians and stroll the boys out of the restaurant. I have to protect my babies at all costs. There is no telling what might happen if they fight again. As I walk away from the table, I overhear Eric say something to Sage and Kevin.

Eric states, "Guys, let's settle this with proper decorum. Now is not the time or place to hash this out. On top of that, the manager is on the phone and may be calling the police."

I see Sage step away from Kevin. Sage doesn't take his eye off of them as he walks out of the restaurant. He catches up to me as I put the boys in the car. Sage gives the boys a goodbye hug and lets me know he'll contact me later. He heads to his car and drives off. As I pull off, I see Kevin and Eric walking out of the restaurant conversing.

CHAPTER 11
Eric's Perspective

"Eric, you should have punched Sage in the back of the head instead of telling us to stop. I guess if you saw the manager on the phone, you played it smart," Kevin says.

"No, we didn't need to pummel that idiot. I didn't see the manager on the phone either. Kevin, we have to think this situation through with our minds. Force will not rectify this situation for us. We have to be tactful," I orate.

"Man, what are you talking about? How is being tactful going to help us?" Kevin asks.

"Here's what I'm saying. Imagine that the boys aren't ours. I know we don't want to, but we have to consider that possibility. I'm saying we should be tactful because we will need to have something in place to cover our backs in that instance," I narrate.

"I get that, but if they're not our kids, we have no options. The way I see it, we can beat Sage's ass every time we see him. I know I'll be mad enough to fight him repeatedly," Kevin verbalizes.

"That's a terrible choice because there's too much effort in that. We can't afford to fight in the streets everyday like some two-bit thugs. I'm telling you that will never work," I indicate.

Kevin asks, "Well, what do you have in mind, since you're so tactful? What can we do to help our situation?"

"Do you love Devin? Will you protect him to the bitter end?" I inquire.

"That's one dumb ass question. You know I love my boy to death. Don't ask me questions that you know the answers to," Kevin replies. "Get to your point."

"Right, so you love your boy and I love mine. We have that established, so let's build on it. If we find out that we're not the fathers, I'm not willing to never see Deric again and I'm willing to do anything to keep that from happening," I voice.

"Well, we won't have a choice, but to comply with the rulings of the law," Kevin says.

"I'm glad you mention the law because I agree with some of that and some I disagree with. If you don't know, when the boys were born I signed their birth certificates, so legally I'm their father. The only people who will refute that is

Sheena and Sage if the results come back negative for us being the dads. Now, if something happened to Sheena and Sage, nobody would be able to question paternity to take the boys from us. The world knows that we both have a child, so things would just continue on that way except no Sheena. You can raise Devin and I'll raise Deric. They'll play together and do the things they've been doing together all along," I explain.

"Oh, I see where you are going with this. We get Sage and Sheena out of the picture and then we have the boys to ourselves. That's real devious and demented. You're talking about murder. Murder is totally different than a scuffle or two," Kevin acknowledges.

"I know, but I'm tired of being played by Sheena. Now, she wants to take my only love from me. She can't do that to me. Deric is my life," I assert.

"I understand that you're angry right now, but you'll calm down later. Your feelings are commandeering your rational thought. You can't be serious about committing a double homicide. I can't get on board with this. We can get caught and go to jail," Kevin expresses.

"I'm not irrational. My mind is as clear as a summer's day. The likelihood of us getting caught is slim to none. It's all in the planning. We can be each other's alibis if need be," I state.

Kevin speaks, "This is unreal. I can't believe I'm having a conversation about killing Sheena.

This is too much for me."

"Listen, you told me that you burned the lounge down and you didn't get caught. That's because the plan was flawless. Additionally, you had Sage as the scapegoat," I verbalize.

Kevin talks, "Yeah, I got away with it because of the scapegoat, but we don't have a scapegoat in this case. We'll be the prime suspects. Especially me, since I had that fight with Sage at In the Mix."

"You'll easily be eliminated as a suspect once I serve as an alibi for you. Besides, if we do it right, we won't even have to worry about alibis. Don't forget that Sage has many enemies. He got shot at In the Mix years ago and recently his lounge was burned down. If an investigation was cast, they would have too many suspects to follow," Eric communicates.

"I see where you're coming from. It makes sense that we could get away with it, but I'm just not sure about it. It's just a lot to lose. We could go to jail if we get caught," Kevin mentions.

"Well, just think about it. Hopefully, we won't have to go that route. If luck is on our side, we'll get these tests done and we'll be confirmed as being the fathers," I say.

"Okay, I'll let you know, but I'm leaning against it. Set up the paternity test with Sheena. Man, I'm too upset to even talk to her right now, let alone see her," Kevin voices.

"Cool, I'll set it up for next week," I reply.

We part ways and look forward to getting the paternity tests performed. I decide to call Sheena to set up the day and time for the tests. I can't help but think how my son may be snatched away from me. I don't care what the DNA test reveals because I love Deric. I've only known him to be my son, so that's all that matters to me. I have friends who I love like brothers even though there's no blood relation and this is no different. I love Deric no matter what.

Days have gone past and I haven't heard from Sheena or seen my son. I don't know if I can cope. I want to see him now, but all I have are pictures to look at. They provide a small degree of solace for me. I look on Sheena's Instagram page and see pictures of Deric and Devin from earlier today. I'm livid that I'm not there to see him. I'm even more upset that Sage is in some of the pictures holding my son. The anger I have is boiling inside of me. It's late and I need to get some sleep.

The next morning I wake up and get ready for work. I open up my Instagram page to get a glimpse of Deric on Sheena's page, but to my horror, she's blocked me as a friend. Now, I can't see current pictures of my boy. I only want to see pictures of him because I miss him and now I can't even do that. What a fucking bitch she is! She isn't worthy of someone as precious as Deric. Sage doesn't deserve to breathe the same air as my son. I could walk up to Sage and choke the life out of his body with my bare hands right now. I take a double shot of Hennessey to settle my nerves.

I go to work like normal, but today is a crappy day. It started off wrong and now there's no correcting it. I've been snapping at my secretary and teachers all morning. The drink I had calmed my nerves slightly, but clearly not completely. I think I need to leave work before I hurt someone's feelings here. I take an early lunch and go to the mall to get Deric a teddy bear. I'll take it to the daycare and see him for a few minutes. That'll surely make me feel better.

I go to the mall and find the perfect bear. After I leave the mall, I head to the daycare. I walk into the daycare and the attendant greets me. She's smiling from ear to ear. I don't know her, so I have no clue as to why she's smiling at me.

"You're going to make somebody's day with that teddy bear," she comments.

I reply, "Thanks. That's the plan. I'm here for Deric Mills. I'm not picking him up; I'm just here to see him for a minute and give him this bear."

"Sure. Let me get your name and identification and I'll let you back," she voices.

I give her my driver's license and she verifies my name on Deric's contact list. She looks it over several times as if she's confused. It never takes this long for me to see Deric. The process is normally very short. Hell, she only has to look at a sheet of paper to make sure my name is on it.

I don't know what the holdup is.

"Ma'am is everything alright?" I ask.

"Well, not quite sir. I'm looking at this list of contacts to pick Deric up and you're not on it. I'm sorry, but I can't allow you to see him," the lady says.

"Ma'am, you must be mistaken. I'm the boy's father, so I know I'm on the list and I've picked my son up several times before. You need to call someone who knows what the hell they're doing," I state.

She replies, "I don't appreciate your vulgar language. Sir, you can't see him. I don't have you listed as being able to see him, so you'll have to leave now before I call the police."

"You evil bitch! You wouldn't dare call the cops on me and all I'm trying to do is see my son. I guess women don't really care if men see their children," I comment.

"Sir, I won't stoop to your level of ignorance, but I'm calling the police in thirty seconds if you don't leave immediately," she informs.

I can't believe they're treating me like this. They clearly have made a mistake and now I'm paying the price for it. This is totally unacceptable. I'm going to ask if I can talk to a manager. To my good fortune, the manager hears the commotion and comes from her office to the front desk.

"Is there a problem here? What's the reason for the noise up here?" the manager asks.

"Ma'am, I apologize for making so much noise, but I'm trying to see my son and your attendant isn't allowing me, so I'm just a little frustrated," I assert.

"Come into my office, so we can get to the bottom of this and clear the confusion," says the manager.

We enter the manager's office and attempt to clear up what's going on. She pulls up Deric's file and sees that I used to be a contact on his paperwork. Now, I'm no longer on his paperwork. She informs me that Sheena changed the documents a couple of days back. I'm more than furious about the news I'm receiving, but I can't take my frustrations out on the workers here. I catch a quick glance of the paperwork and I can see that Sage is now listed as the father of the boys. There is no way Sheena is getting away with this bullshit.

She's pushed me to the point of no return. I've tried to be patient and understanding through all of the twists and turns of our relationship, but that hasn't paid off. They say nice guys finish last, but not this time. I'm a man on a mission and I refuse to lose.

"I appreciate your willingness to give me clarity on this situation, but I have one more question for you," I voice.

"Sure no problem," she says. "Ask away."

"How is it possible for Sheena to change the paperwork without me being aware of the changes?" I ask.

"We get these types of questions and situations all the time. Miss Mills is the one who originally enrolled the boys into this daycare, so she has the ultimate authority on who is listed on the paperwork as visitors, contacts, and whatever else pertains to her children," she explains.

"Oh, I understand the process. Thanks, for your help," I say as I exit her office.

On the way out, I apologize to the lady at the front desk. I really am sorry for the way I spoke to her. I'm even sorrier that I made such a big scene in here. I don't want anyone to consider me as a possible suspect when I hurt Sheena. You better believe that I'm going to hurt that sinister bitch.

I walk back to the car and take a minute to calm down. My nerves are shot to the point where my hands won't stop shaking. I'm the kettle, my blood is water, and the whistle is blaring through the kitchen. Unfortunately, I have to go back to school to attend an expulsion hearing, so I can't dip on work for the rest of the day. On the way back to the school, I call Kevin to tell him that Sheena no longer has us listed as the boys' parents at the daycare.

"Hello," Kevin says.

"What's up man? Do you have a moment to chat?" I ask.

"Yeah, I'm good for a few minutes. What's up?" Kevin asks.

"Well, I went to the daycare to see Deric and they wouldn't let me see him. Sheena has taken both of our names off of the paperwork, so now we can't go up there to pick the boys up or even see them," I report.

"I wouldn't expect anything different from her. You know how she does. Man, don't sweat it. It's all games with her. She's just pushing buttons. Let it go," Kevin narrates.

"No, this is more than pushing buttons. I caught a glimpse of the files on the boys and she even switched the paperwork to reflect Sage as being the father," I tell.

Kevin speaks, "I guess she's willing to go all the way with this thing. It's a shame that she's doing us like this. Don't worry; she'll meet her karma one day."

"She'll meet a harsh fate if you're willing to help me. I'm telling you it's simple. We can have the boys forever," I comment.

"Goodbye, I'm not talking about this anymore. You'll have to do that one on your own. I'll find another way to get my son. Murder isn't an option," Kevin orates.

"Maybe not for you it isn't, but for me, it's the only option if this test doesn't come back in my favor," I assert.

"I hear you, but I won't be a part of it," Kevin replies.

We end the call as I pull up to the school. I attend the expulsion meeting and finish the school day with evil deeds on my mind. I have to be honest and admit that I'm upset with Kevin. I am really shocked that he's unwilling to conspire with me to get this done. Maybe he doesn't love Devin as much as I love Deric. He's normally the angry and aggressive one, but not this time. Unfortunately, I'm leading in that department. I can't pull this off alone.

It's time for the paternity tests to be taken. The last few days have been filled with anger and frustration, but I haven't shown it one bit. I need to pretend as if nothing is wrong just in case I need to get violent. I don't want anyone remembering that I've been acting differently lately. I get showered up and dressed and head to the paternity test location. I see Kevin's car in the parking lot when I arrive.

Moments after I walk inside, Sheena comes in with the boys. I greet her, but my attention is on my son. As soon as Deric sees my face, he gives me the biggest smile ever. My boy knows who his father is. I feel a whole lot better now that I'm seeing him. Not being able to see him has made me feel like I was missing limbs. I pick him up out of his stroller and hug him.

"Daddy has missed you son. You just don't know how much. Daddy loves you more than air itself," I say.

Kevin is just as infatuated with Devin as I am with Deric. Our sons have us like putty in their hands. I will savor this moment because I don't know when I'll get it again. We eventually head back to the testing room and handle what we came to handle. Sheena is all business and is behaving as Kevin and I really don't matter to her. It actually seems like we never mattered to her. She is colder than an ice cube, but it's fine with me because I'm not feeling her. I'm only here for my boy.

After the test, we leave the facility. The test was fairly quick and they said the results will be back in two business days. That's not a long amount of time in theory, but I'm dreading the wait. This is the most important news of my life. I wish I could speed up time to get the results back, but I can't. I guess I'll just have to wait.

CHAPTER 12
Eric's Perspective

Well, it's been a very stressful and nerve-wracking week to say the least. The paternity test results took a little longer than expected to come back. My patience wore thin, but I got through the wait. Unfortunately, the results revealed what I hoped they wouldn't. I am not the biological father of Deric and Kevin is not biological father of Devin.

I can't even lie and say it doesn't hurt. I'm emotionally torn and severely depressed. Now, Sheena has banned me and Kevin from seeing the boys and it's in my best interest to let it be for now. I'm okay with losing the battle, so I can win the war. I'm all about the end result. My end result is having Sheena and Sage permanently out of the way, so I can have Deric with me.

I can't believe Kevin is taking this as lightly

as he is. He claims he's also devastated, but he surely isn't acting like it. I guess we all handle things differently. I'm okay with that because I handle things the way I deem necessary too.

That's why I'm sitting outside of Sheena's house right now. I need to catch a glimpse of my son. Hopefully, I can see her pulling him out of the car. She'll be pulling up any minute now unless she had an errand to run after picking the boys up. Shit, for all I know, she could have had Sage pick them up from daycare. Nonetheless, I'll just wait it out. Besides, I really have no other option, but to wait it out. I can't get my plan fully underway without accessing her garage. I purchased a garage door opener from the home improvement store, so I'll be able to access her garage when I need to. For this reason, I have to get in there to program the garage door opener.

Finally, Sheena pulls up three hours later. I've been waiting for hours in this damn car for her to arrive. Where the hell was she? I'm so fucking angry right now. It looks like she's pulling the car into the garage. Damn, I won't be able to fulfill this craving I have to see him.

I should just rush Sheena while she's in the garage, hit her over the head, and take my son. D.C. is a tough place to live and it could seem like a random act of violence. Sheena doesn't immediately close the garage door behind her. Instead, she pulls one of the boys out of the car and runs him in the house.

This is my chance. I don't know which boy she took inside, but this is my opportunity to get inside the garage. I'll let her close the garage door and then pounce on her like a lion pounces on its prey. I get out of my car and run inside of the garage. I duck down behind some boxes Sheena has stacked along the wall.

Sheena comes back to the garage, but doesn't take the remaining child out of the car. Instead, she goes to check the mail. As soon as she comes back with the mail and lets the door down, she's going to be under siege like Steven Segal. I build up my nerves to get in attack mode. I summon up anger from all past experiences in my life to this point. I'm a raging bull. No, I'm an erupting volcano.

Perfect, Sheena is walking back with her head down as she reviews the pieces of mail she's received. Sheena is completely oblivious to her surroundings and imminent demise. As she crosses the threshold of the garage, she hits the garage door opener and the door begins to close.

I slowly and quietly ease from behind the boxes to get close to Sheena before I attack her. A couple of punches to the back of her head followed by me viciously choking her will be simple as pie. She literally won't know what hit her. Sheena stops at the car to get Deric out. The garage door is almost completely down, so I begin to make my move.

I'm almost behind Sheena as she takes Deric

out of his car seat when headlights shine into the remaining opening of the garage door and then a horn blares. I tuck back into my former hiding spot. I hope I wasn't detected by the visitor. Sheena looks back and hits the garage door opener and the door begins to open back up. There is no way whoever that is saw me.

Clearly, Sheena was expecting whoever this person is. Seconds later I hear Ilesha's voice. I would have been caught for sure. Ilesha could have walked up on me while I was killing Sheena and called the cops. Even if I hadn't killed her yet, I still would have been arrested for assault and breaking and entering. Hell, the authorities may have even charged me with attempted murder. If Ilesha had interrupted while I was in the act of killing Sheena, I would have had to kill her too. I definitely need Kevin to help me pull this off. He has to get onboard with this for it to work. If not Kevin, I need another person to be on my team. I hate knowing I have a fool proof plan, but can't implement it.

"Damn, girl! You didn't have to shut the garage door in my face. You knew I was right behind your ass," Ilesha remarks.

"I thought you stopped or something. It took you long enough to get here. I wasn't gonna wait all night to close the garage door. I gave you enough time as is," Sheena replies.

"Girl, don't act brand new like you don't know I move at my own speed. Ain't nothing new here," Ilesha says.

Sheena speaks, "I know you do and so do I. That's why I was closing the damn door. You were not about to have me waiting around for you like I used to do lame ass Kevin and Eric. Their asses are so tired."

Sheena picks Deric up and they walk into the house while they laugh at the expense of Kevin and me. They think it's funny to treat men poorly. Well, that's okay. I'll have my laugh when this is all over. Fortunately, Sheena doesn't have a free hand to let the garage door down and doesn't ask Ilesha to let it down because they leave the door open. I'm able to slide out of the garage undetected. I drive to Kevin's house to talk to him once more about helping me with my cabal. I get to his place and ring the doorbell. He lets me in and we converse for a while.

"So, you mean to tell me that you're not going to do anything about Sheena taking our sons from us?" I inquire.

"Man, I'm just as sick as you over this, if not sicker. I want to strangle Sheena and Sage for having us go through this turmoil, but I'm not risking my freedom over this," Kevin explains.

"We're not going to jail over this. You are too scared. Besides, we have to get back at them for this. We can't just sit back and let them have bliss," I voice.

Kevin replies, "It's just not for me. The possibility of prison just doesn't sit well with me.

I'm not your guy."

"Sheena played you good. You say you're afraid of jail, but you went along with Sheena's plan to burn down the lounge. You could have easily went to jail for arson," I report.

"That was different because her plan was solid. There wasn't any way I could get caught. I loved every second of watching that bitch go up in flames too," Kevin verbalizes.

"We can put together a solid plan too. She's no smarter than we are. All we have to do is plan this out and our sons will be ours. Yeah, it was good seeing the lounge burnt to a crisp, but too bad it was short lived," I vocalize.

"Why do you say it was short lived?" Kevin asks.

"I say short lived because In the Mix is being rebuilt as we speak. Come on, bro. You had to know that. All of D.C. has been talking about it," I tell.

"You are shitting me! You're telling me that because you want me to get onboard with your scheme. I was born at night, but it wasn't last night. Good try with that one," Kevin utters.

"Now, why would I lie about something that can be easily verified? Do you wanna ride over there now and take a look for yourself?" I ask.

"Let's go," Kevin replies.

We drive to the lounge and Kevin sees the newly constructed portions of the building. He is perturbed at this new found information. I'm glad he is upset because he may be more willing to help with my plan to take my son back.

"No need to be mad that Sheena played you. It's just what she does. She had you burn down the lounge, so he could get a new one. It's probably gonna be bigger and better," I narrate.

"I can't believe this shit! Take me to her damn house right now," Kevin orders.

"We don't need to go to her house. You're upset and will only cause a scene. The last thing we need is a scene. That'll be more scrutiny on us if we move forward with the plan," I say.

"The hell with your plan! I'm not doing it, so it really doesn't matter. I just need to let her tell me face to face what's going on with the lounge," Kevin states.

Against my better judgment I drive to Sheena's house. Kevin jumps out of the car before it even stops rolling. He zooms up her steps, rings the doorbell, and pounds on the door. Ilesha opens the door and questions Kevin angrily.

"Why the hell are you over here banging on the door like you ain't got no damn sense?" inquires Ilesha.

"This has nothing to do with you Ilesha and I damn sure don't have to answer to you about why I'm at a house that's not yours," Kevin replies sternly.

Kevin pushes past Ilesha and dashes inside the house. She turns in after Kevin grabbing his arm in an attempt to stop him, but her efforts are futile. Kevin accidentally flings Ilesha to the floor when he pulls away from her. I fly up the steps and go in the house to see the drama unfold. He seems to be in combat mode even though he claimed he wasn't going to make a scene.

"What's all the commotion?" Sheena asks as she appears at the top of the stairs.

"Kevin bulldozed his ass in here and is about to get cut the fuck up!" screams Ilesha as she gets up off the floor.

"What in the hell are you two doing here? Don't you know that you have no place in here anymore? And did you just throw Ilesha to the floor?" Sheena asks angrily.

Ilesha stands up and pushes Kevin as he walks up the stairs toward Sheena. He falls face forward onto the steps and Ilesha hits him upside his head and back. Sheena springs down the stairs and grabs Kevin's hand as he turns to strike Ilesha. Ilesha lands a couple more blows to the side of Kevin's face before I pull her off of him. Kevin lunges for Ilesha, but I put her behind me to keep Kevin from getting her. Sheena yells for us to leave her house before she calls the cops.

Kevin won't stop trying to get to Ilesha for anything. He wants to hurt her badly, but I refuse to let him. We have bigger fish to fry than Ilesha. Unfortunately, Ilesha wants to get at Kevin too. I don't think I'll be able to hold them back much longer. Sheena, Ilesha, and Kevin are all screaming at the top of their lungs. The screaming comes to an end when the boys start crying uncontrollably. I guess all of the clamor has startled them. They all calm down immediately and Sheena goes to check on them. She's quickly able to calm the boys down and comes back downstairs.

"The reason I'm here is because I noticed the lounge is being rebuilt. You know why that shocked me, so I figured I'd see what you know about it," Kevin explains.

Sheena replies, "Yes, it's being rebuilt. I felt it was in the best interest of the boys to allow Sage to file the insurance claim and get the lounge up and running."

Kevin speaks, "I stuck my neck out for you and this is what I get for it. I knew I should've let you handle it yourself. Let's face it, you're worried about what's in the best interest for you and your boo Sage."

"Well, I'm sorry you feel that way, but this is how it is. For the record, Sage and I aren't a couple, so you need to stop saying it. He's the father of my children, so I do want him to be financially stable," Sheena expresses.

"Cut that father of your children shit out! We've been those boys' fathers since their first breath. Please don't disrespect us like that," I chime in.

"Hell, you may have been, but you aren't anymore. You both have the test results, so your daddy days are over," comments Ilesha.

"That may be the case, but Sage's daddy days will be short lived," Kevin remarks.

I know he isn't referring to me wanting to kill Sage. He wouldn't be dumb enough to reveal what I told him in confidence. That would surely kill my plan. I know he isn't the sharpest pencil in the box, but he can't be totally without a brain.

"What are you talking about? Why would his time as a father be short lived?" Sheena asks.

"You know what I'm talking about. Well, last I checked, you set it up to look like Sage burnt down his own lounge to collect insurance money. If you proceed with allowing him to rebuild, I'll have to drop a dime to D.C.'s finest about all of this," Kevin informs.

"Umm, that wouldn't be a smart move on your part. Don't forget that you're the one who actually did it," Sheena voices.

"Yeah, I hear you, but like I said before, everything points to Sage," Kevin speaks.

"Let's replay this for a moment. One, you actually did it. Two, I'll testify that Sage was with me the entire night making love to me. Three, you sent me a text stating that you burned the lounge down. Lastly, I had you get gas that night and I know it wouldn't be too hard to tip a cop off to that. You are definitely on tape somewhere filling up the red gas can," Sheena expresses.

"Sounds like she rammed your dick in your ass with that response," states Ilesha. "And don't forget that Sage whooped your fucking ass at the lounge shortly before it was burnt down, so there's motive right there."

"It doesn't have to come to all of that. He just wanted an explanation is all. Kevin, tell her it's all good and no hard feelings," I say.

"You gotta be kidding me. I know your conniving ass ain't gonna try to pin this shit on me. I underestimated how much of a bitch you really are!" Kevin screams.

Ilesha shoots back, "She's a bad, bad bitch. Get it right."

"Damn right! And one other thing... Get the fuck outta my house! Both of you need to get to stepping now!" Sheena dictates.

I pull Kevin to the door and we exit Sheena's house. We get in the car and he can't stop throwing punches in the air. It's like he's having a boxing match except there's no opponent in front of him. I decide to add fuel to the fire.

"Sheena's gonna send your ass to jail man. That's real fucked up of her," I voice.

"No, she's not gonna get the chance to do that. She'll be dead before that happens. I don't know your plan to get them out of this world, but I'm all ears. They'll die before I go to jail. Fuck it, I'm down with killing them and we'll get the boys. It's a win-win situation for us," Kevin speaks.

"Great! I'm glad you're onboard. I couldn't do it without you," I vocalize.

"Cool, what do you have in mind? You wanna loosen up the tires on their cars?" Kevin inquires.

"No, we have to come up with something a bit more creative than that," I reply. "I have unimpeded access to Sheena's house, so let's talk."

CHAPTER 13
Sheena's Perspective

Last night got crazy. The last thing I expected was for Kevin and Eric to show up at my house. Things got pretty bad, but at least nobody got hurt even though Kevin did put his hands on Ilesha. I still can't believe he did that. Tense situations like last night don't normally end well for at least one person and if it were up to Ilesha, Kevin would have been on the receiving end of a bad night. I'm glad my house wasn't damaged in all of the mayhem. Needless to say, somebody would have been going to court if that were the case.

Sage and Rachel couldn't believe what happened when I told them the story. Sage and Rachel both agree that Kevin is a coward. Sage wants to go find Kevin and beat him up like he did once before. I urge him not to do so. Let's be real; he's a father of twins and he doesn't need to chase people down in the streets like we live in the Wild West.

Instead, I implore him to stay focused on getting the lounge back up and running, so my girls and I will have our hangout back. To be honest, I do want Sage to start making that boatload of cash he was once making too. He's actually been such a sweetheart to me lately and he's been nothing other than a perfect father to the boys. He takes them to daycare and picks them up daily.

I'm glad because it's one less thing on my plate to worry about. Additionally, Sage is catching up on missed time with the boys. That's extremely important to me and him. Sage and I are also getting close like we once were. I'm surprisingly entertaining the idea of me and Sage being a couple again.

I love the way he takes care of my sons. It really turns me on to see a man stand up and handle his business. We've been on a few dates, since the paternity tests, but we haven't had sex. He wants me badly, but I want to take it slow. I don't want my decision to date him again to be clouded by sex. Sage always offers to eat me out because he knows that normally leads to sex, but I've even declined those requests. I'm using this time to build our relationship. Sex will come later. I have to admit that it's not easy to resist because the kitty cat is throbbing. My girls are loving as always and my boys are healthy and getting bigger by the minute. Business is even going very well. All facets of my life are finally falling into place.

After visiting Rachel, I stop on the way home to get something to eat. I'll have my boys home in no time. I know they're sleepy. Hell, I'm a tad bit sleepy myself. Seems like I've been running around all day long. Well, I guess I have been. I stopped by the office, then Sage's, after that Rachel's, and now I'm finally heading home. Talk about a full day.

I pull up to the house and hit the garage door button. Unfortunately, the door doesn't open. I must not have hit it hard enough, so I hit it again. Damn, it didn't open again. I hope the battery in my fob went dead and not something more serious. I don't have time to wait for the garage door repairman to come service it.

I pull into my driveway and grab Deric out of his car seat. I lug him up the steps, open the door to the house, and drop him in the foyer. I run back outside and repeat the same procedure with Devin. Damn I'm out of shape. Carrying these boys up the steps has bust my ass. Time to get my boys changed and ready for bed.

After I put the boys to bed, I do a few things around the house and get myself ready for bed as well. I'm exhausted and fall asleep relatively quickly. I'm awakened shortly after falling asleep, by the sound of something moving in the house.

I don't know exactly where the sound came from, but I get up to check on the boys.

I go into their room and look them over. Thankfully, they're sleeping comfortably. I go downstairs to see if everything's okay down there. I creep downstairs and investigate what's going on. I wish I had a weapon of some sort, but I don't. I'm tripping for sure.

I have all of the lights on and I don't see anything wrong in the house, but I feel someone's presence. The weird thing is that nothing is amiss. Why is the closet door partially open? I go to the kitchen and grab the largest knife I can find. I stand at the door and build up my nerve.

"Come out of the closet now before I come in after you," I order. "I have a weapon and will use it on you if you don't exit the closet now!"

The room remains quiet and no motion comes out of the closet. I will count to ten and then I'm going into the closet. I can't let whoever is in the closet determine when he or she wants to come out and attack me and my children. I open the door swiftly, let out a scream, and charge into the closet with the knife in front of me.

To my embarrassment, there's nobody in my closet but me. I managed to stab my favorite coat with the knife. I chuckle and put the knife back in the kitchen. What the hell was I thinking? I'm scaring myself to death. I go back upstairs and check on the boys before I head back to bed. They're still resting and I need to do the same.

Back to bed I go.

The next morning, Sage comes to get the boys to take them to daycare. I tell him about the noise I heard last night and that I found nothing disturbed in the house. He laughed at me after I told him how I stabbed my coat to death. I'm not surprised that Sage laughed because I thought it was funny too.

"You're obviously under too much stress, otherwise you wouldn't be acting like that. You haven't been on vacation, a real vacation in quite some time. All you've been doing is taking care of the boys, worrying about your personal affairs, and working. I also think you need to release and I don't mean a drink," Sage speaks.

"I have been going through it, but contrary to what you believe, I don't need dick. Thank you very much. I'm fine, so get your mind out of the gutter. Men always think the answer to every woman's problems is some dick. Well, that's the wrong answer," I reply.

"Are you saying some dick and an orgasm wouldn't make you feel better? Is that what you want me to believe?" Sage inquires.

I ask, "Okay, okay. Are you gonna take care of it for me?"

Sage inquires as he moves in closer to me, "Take care of what?"

I step even closer to Sage and reply, "Take care of the boys' dirty diapers and bottles."

"Oh, you got jokes. You know that's not what

you want me to take care of. You acting like that thing isn't ready for me. I can tell you want it from the way your sweet spot was drenched in the car on the way to Jersey," Sage utters.

"Umm, I wasn't wet. It was hot in the car and I was sweating a lot that day. The heat was up way too high in the car," I shoot back.

"Now that's some bullshit. You can admit that my advances still make you weak in the knees like SWV. It's cool because the only woman's touch I've ever craved is yours," Sage voices.

Sage eases up on me and pulls me to his chest. I act like I'm pulling away, but I'm really not. Sage rubs my arms slowly and I feel comforted. I pull away again and turn my back to Sage. This time Sage grabs me from behind and kisses me gently in the center of the back of my neck. I feel his full, soft, and juicy lips on me and they send chills down my spine. The placement of his kiss is an aphrodisiac and I'm instantly turned on.

He kisses me again in the same spot except this time he adds the perfect amount of tongue action to it. Then he slides his tongue across my neck to my ear. My body temperature begins to rise. Sage gropes my back and gives me a massage while we stand. He places his hands under my shirt and continues massaging my back. Sage stops addressing my back and turns me around and gazes into my eyes. His soft brown eyes are dreamy. I'm lost in them and I can't get over how heavenly his strong muscular arms feel around me. I feel like I've never felt them before.

I can tell by the seductive look in Sage's eyes that his hormones are raging and he wants me. Furthermore, I can tell by the bulge in his pants that he wants to fuck me fast and hard. I lick my lips slowly and sensually while gazing back at him because I want him to fuck me right here and now. I know he doesn't deserve to have me, but I want to feel his dart pierce my bull's eye profusely. Maybe it's because he's a forbidden fruit that I want to taste over and over again.

He rubs my inner thigh and I pull away. He then gropes it forcefully. I feel my pussy throb and release a small gush of moisture. I love his strong hand on my leg. Sage slides his hand up and down my thigh subtly and my pussy gets wetter. I pant and begin to breathe heavily. Sage can tell I like his advances because I spread my legs wide open, so he can have clear access to my hot box. Sage doesn't hesitate one nanosecond to fondle my pussy. To my delight, Sage puts his hand inside of my leggings and panties and starts to massage my clit. I'm breathing even more intensely than before. This feeling is magical and we're just getting started. He sticks two of his fingers inside of my gushing pool of pleasure and I gyrate on his fingers just like I was riding his dick.

"You like that?" Sage asks as he leans in and kisses my collar bone.

"Yes," I moan.

What Sage does next turns me on even more and makes my pussy spurt with moisture like Niagara Falls. Sage is such a freak. He keeps one finger in me rubbing my G-spot and rubs my clit with the other. He then begins to rub my nipple ever so slightly through my shirt. The gentle sensation on my nipple has my legs getting weak. I'm biting my bottom lip because the feeling is euphoric. He takes his finger out of my pussy and off my clit. He raises his hand to his face and I see my juices streaming down his fingers. Sage sucks all of my juices off of his fingers like he's devouring an ice cream cone.

"You taste delicious and you're absolutely ravishing. I want to taste you more. I wanna taste that sweet thang you got between your legs," Sage says in a low sexy voice.

I pull Sage to the staircase out the line of sight of the boys. I pull one of my legs out of my pants and sit on the staircase. I fondle Sage's dick from the outside of his pants and then unzip his pants. I pull his dick out and begin licking his head. Sage's eyes are rolling in the back of his head as he grabs my shoulders and slowly strokes my mouth with his rock solid dick. I grip his dick with one hand and with the other I play with myself. I angle his dick to the side of my mouth, so every time he reenters, it looks like his dick is going to poke out of my jaw. He goes crazy and moans every time I repeat the motion. I pop Sage's dick out of my mouth with a loud sucking noise.

Sage seizes the opportunity to eat my pussy by dropping down to his knees, ripping my panties off, and sticking his tongue inside of me. I moan as I feel the heat from his breath and the sensation of his tongue lashing my pussy. Sage eats like a champion and has my coochie so wet that my juices are flowing from my pussy down my ass.

"Fuck yeah!" I scream as I massage his head in a circular motion around my clit.

The air is filled with the scent of sex and the sounds of slurping noises as he devours my kitty cat. I can't take anymore. My body is inundated with pleasure, so I attempt to run from his tongue, only I can't. It's not that I don't want to, but it's because I'm pinned down on the stairs. Sage has me locked in and all I can do is take whatever he delivers.

"Put him in. I need to feel him in me now," I order.

Sage isn't moving fast enough for me. He continues to eat my pussy even after my demands for him to fuck me. I know he just likes to see me squirm, but I want to fuck, so I push his head from between my legs and begin reaching for his cock.

"You wanna feel my dick, huh? How do you want it?" Sage asks.

I answer, "I want it any way you wanna give it to me. I just want it hard and for you to get to the bottom of it."

"I'm gonna get to the bottom of your pussy like a sunken ship gets to the bottom of the ocean floor," Sage guarantees.

I'm done with talking. Sage enters my pussy straight forward. He's like an airplane coming into landing positon straight on. My pussy is tight and I can feel it gripping his dick. I feel Sage's dick pulsing inside of me as if he's cumming on every stroke, but he's not. Desire is in his eyes and lust is in the air. Sage has one hand behind my neck and is pulling my body toward him as he pokes me with his rod. My pussy is gushing wet and farts as he thrusts me. My ass is rubbing the stairs so much that it's beginning to hurt, so I put my hands under me and raise myself up. Now, Sage has an even straighter shot to my pussy and is able to go deeper inside of me.

It's like he's in a mine and has just discovered new pussy because Sage is pounding me harder and harder. His dick is a hammer and my pussy is the head on the nail. I scream... I moan... I fuck him back. Hell, I don't know what to do. I massage my clit as he waves his magic wand inside of me. I run my fingers through my hair. I grab my stomach because it feels like he's fucking me through my belly button. I'm sweating, my body is tingling, and I'm cumming all over his dick. That release has my body drooping like a wilted flower on the staircase. Sage lifts my legs and places them behind my head. My pussy is wide open for the ramming and he does exactly that.

Sage slaps his dick on my pussy and then proceeds to ram his rod into my hot box. He grunts like a barbarian as he serves me the meat. I'm a bad girl and Sage is punishing me. His dick is so deep inside of me that I want to put my hands on him to keep him from penetrating me so deeply, but I'm a grown ass woman, so I don't. I have to take the beating I asked for. Sage's balls slap my sweet spot like a drummer slaps his drum set. Sage's strokes are faster, shorter, and more powerful, so I know he's about to nut. I contract my pussy muscles while he strokes me.

"Baby... Baby... Shit, I'm cummin!!! Ahhhhh!!!" Sage screams.

Sage pulls out of me and begins stroking his dick. A second later, several large gushes of cum rocket out of his dick. Some lands on my shirt, pussy, and my legs. He has made a total mess of me, but I don't mind because the amount of nut present tells me that he hasn't been fucking anyone else. I grab his dick and start stroking it while I lick his head. He squirms because his head is sensitive and the feeling is too much to endure. Payback's a bitch. I slurp and swallow all of the excess nut being released from his dick. He pulls back and falls to the floor.

I'm very weak and drained from the massive orgasm I just had, but I have to get up. I need to get to the office early and now I have to wash again. I rush Sage up, strip off the rest of my clothes, and beeline to the shower. I exit the shower and throw on an outfit that doesn't need ironing.

"All of their belongings are right there Sage. You need to get them there if you plan on dropping them off," I say.

"You're right. I would keep them with me today, but I can't," Sage replies.

He leaves with the boys and drops them off at the daycare facility. He's going to the lounge to check on the progress being made. Reluctantly, I head to work once Sage leaves with the boys. I arrive at work and walk to my office. My assistant comes in and provides me with updates I asked for. However, I don't quite catch everything she says because I'm zoned out.

I know I'm not crazy, but I think I saw Kevin following me on my way to work this morning. I hope he's not watching me. Well, that wasn't his car, so maybe I'm being paranoid. It wouldn't be the first time I've overreacted to a situation before. Either way, I'm here now, so it's time to get focused and time to get to work.

While, I'm at work I keep getting phone calls transferred to my office line, but nobody is speaking when I answer the call. I call Sage to see if he's been playing on my phone today. He's definitely a prankster, so it's possible that he's messing with me about stabbing my coat last night. Sage tells me that he's not the one making the calls. In fact, he said he got some anonymous calls from someone claiming to be Mr. Reaper and Mr. Grim. Things just got real. Is someone putting death threats out on Sage and harassing me? If so, it's probably Kevin. He's probably mad over the whole Sage situation. Sage is amused by the childish pranks and doesn't think too much of it.

"I don't think this is the least bit funny! I shouldn't be harassed by anybody. I'm gonna call the cops on their asses," I express.

Sage responds, "Slow down. Slow down. You don't have anything to tell the cops. You'll call the cops and tell them that you might be being harassed by someone who you didn't see or somebody you don't know if they called you. I don't think it's worth wasting the cops' time to report nothing."

"I guess you're right. You have a good point, but I know in my heart that it's them being assholes. They seem to be buddy-buddy these days," I convey.

"You're most likely right because all of this started once the paternity results came back. I think it's Kevin because he was extremely irate. Eric was real calm about things. He's probably come to terms with the situation. Either way, we still don't know for sure who it is, so we can't do much anyway," Sage narrates.

"Right. Well, I'll let you go. I have to get back

to work. I'll see you later this evening," I voice.

"Cool, what time do you want me to drop the boys off?" Sage asks.

"I'm going straight home after I leave here at five, so any time after that is fine with me. I'm not going anywhere for the rest of the night," I answer.

Sage says, "Cool, I'll be there."

We hang up the phone and I get back to work. I know Sage told me not to worry about it, but I can't stop thinking about who's calling my phone. I want to call both Kevin and Eric to see if one of them will admit to this nonsense. I guess this is why I expected some backlash from the situation. However, it would have been nice for this to go over without any hiccups. Things only go the way you want in a world of fantasy and this is the real world with real outcomes.

Finally, I leave work and go home. The garage door is still broken, so I park in the driveway and get out of the car. What is that box on my step? I wonder if Sage dropped a gift off for me. I love the bow that's draped over the box. I'm excited and can't wait to get it inside to open it. I pick up the box and attempt to open the door. Damn, where's my house key? I hate having to enter through the front door because I can never quickly find my key.

While I'm looking for my key, I see a strange man jogging down my street. I've never seen him a day in my life. I can't make out his face because he has on a cap. He's definitely Eric's size and he's coming this way! Where is that damn key? Oh my, he is even closer. I hope he doesn't have ill intent. Hell, what is that in his hand? Is that a gun? All this stuff in my purse doesn't make any damn sense. I don't think it's in here because I can't find it. I put my back against the door just in case I have to fight for my life. Hell, my boys need me and I refuse to have them grow up without me. I have my mace in my hand and I'm ready to spray. He's slowing down in front of my house as he gets close to my walkway. I'm scared out of my mind.

"Don't come any closer Eric. I'll spray this mace all in your damn face. I'm not playing with you," I say.

The guy looks over at me and takes his cap off. It's not Eric, but I don't know this man and I definitely don't know why he's slowing down in front of my house. I'm not putting my mace down because they could have sent someone here to harm me.

"Ma'am, please don't spray me. I just need some help. I'm from Columbia, South Carolina and I'm here visiting some family. I decided to go for a jog, but I guess I took a wrong turn. I tried plugging the address into my phone, but the GPS was sending me all over the place," reports the jogger.

"Oh, you know I thought you were a robber. Well, how can I help you?" I ask.

"I kinda figured that. Do you know where K Street is?" he asks.

"Yes, go to the corner, make a right, and go two blocks and make a left and you'll be on K Street," I reply.

The guy runs off in the direction I told him to go. My heart is still beating out of my chest. After seemingly thirty minutes of searching, I find my key and let myself in the house. I really blew that out of proportion. I almost sprayed a guy with mace for needing directions. I really need to calm down. I fix myself a glass of wine and grab my mystery gift. There's a card attached that I didn't initially see. The cards reads, "Especially for you".

I carefully untie the beautiful bow that's with my gift. The box is not heavy, so I know it's not a handbag even though I would love a new one. I shake the box to see if I can tell what's inside, but I can't. Hell, I've had enough of the suspense, so I open the box. To my horror, there are a dozen dead irises in the box. I can't stand the sight of them, so I put the lid back on the box.

Oh, the hell with this shit! I know for sure that it's Kevin or Eric. They know that the iris is my absolute favorite flower. They are taunting me and I'm not going to take it. After I sit the flowers down, I hear a noise. It sounds like glass has been broken. I go to the area of the house where it seems the noise has come from. I see one of the squares has been broken out of the window frame where my back door is and the door is faintly ajar. Seeing the glass on the floor, the door open, and the dead flowers sends a fit of panic and fright through my body. I don't know if someone's in the house or not. I move back to the front of the house to grab my purse, so I can retrieve my phone to call the police.

As I scurry to get my phone, I hear another crashing sound. Someone has grabbed one of my glasses and slammed it against the wall. Shards of glass spread everywhere. I look back over my shoulder and see a man dressed in all black and is covered from head to toe. The intruder is wearing a facemask and even has sunglasses covering his eyes. I can't tell from the contour of the intruder's body if it's Kevin or Eric. Hell, it doesn't matter who it is. I just need to get to my phone to call the authorities.

I run to my purse and grab it. I unlock the front door and attempt to open it, but the perpetrator is already on top of me and slams the door shut. He grabs me by the hair and flings me to the floor. Once I'm on the floor, the intruder dives on top of me. I elbow him in the face and it seems to take some of the fight out of him. I go to elbow him again, but this time he's ready for it. He blocks my attempted blow and knees me in the stomach.

The blow to my stomach knocks the air out of me and my arms go limp. I can barely breathe, but I continue to fight as much as I can. Unfortunately, he knees me again in my stomach and my defenses are severely weakened. The felonious caper begins to choke me. I feel the life seeping from my body. As he chokes me, he shakes my neck violently. It's almost like he wants to break my neck. My eyes are rolling in the back of my head and I feel myself losing consciousness. He lets my neck go and places his mouth close to my ear.

He whispers, "Bitch, I know you like to be choked while you are getting fucked. I'm gonna give you what you want. I'm gonna give you one last fuck before you die today."

He pulls my skirt up and yanks my panties off. Unfortunately, I'm still pretty out of it, so I can't muster any strength to get him off of me. I know it's either Kevin or Eric. I hope I'm able to tell if it's Kevin or Eric raping me from the sensation of his dick. Hell, it may not even matter if he kills me afterwards. What the hell am I going to do? I can't fight, run, or scream. This may be the end of my life right here. The thought of death sends tears streaming down my cheeks. The thought of not seeing my boys grow up saddens me in this moment.

"Don't cry now motherfucker. You know payback's a bitch and you're a bitch. See how Sage feels about finding you dead. You're gonna get my dick in your ass before I kill you," he speaks faintly. "Turn your ass over."

He knees me in my stomach once more and flips me over. I'm lying flat on my stomach and he's mounted on top of me. My skirt is still raised and panties ripped off. I hear him fondling with something, so I assume that it's his belt buckle and jeans. All I can do is scream for help and for him to get off of me.

"I'm gonna rip you a new asshole Sheena. You're gonna need stitches when I'm finished with you, but it's not gonna matter because you'll be dead soon after," he whispers sinisterly.

He really seems to be enjoying this. I can tell the thought of revenge is really exciting him. It's not surprising that he wants to rape me before killing me because he just wants to exert control over me, which is something Kevin nor Eric ever had. Next, I feel a disgusting feeling on my ass. He is smacking his dick on my butt cheeks. After that, I hear the sound of him spitting. He must be ready to sodomize me and needed some lubrication.

"This'll be over before you know it. I know you bitches like it rough sometimes and this is gonna be exactly that," he mumbles.

We're still very close to the front door. I use the last bit of strength I have to try to kick the door. Maybe someone will hear my kicks and come to my rescue. Simultaneously, I feel the door knock against my feet. Someone has opened the door. How could somebody have heard my kick that quickly? I barely touched the door. It was more of a brush against the door as opposed to a kick.

"It's only me baby. My bad Sheena. I didn't mean to hit you with the door," Sage says. "But I am carrying the boys, so it'd be nice if you would open the door all the way."

It's Sage and his voice has never sounded so heavenly! He's here to drop the boys off for the night. I forgot all about that once the attack started. The assaulter immediately jumps up off of me and makes a beeline for the kitchen. He's moving faster than a bolt of lightning getting out of here. Sage thinks I'm blocking the door because I just happened to be by the door when he attempted to open it. Sage nudges the door again and peaks inside. To his dismay, he sees me lying almost lifeless on the floor.

He pushes himself all the way in the house, sits the boys down, and draws his gun. He points it around and then drops to his knees to check on me. He flips me over and can tell that I'm still alive. I'm gaining a little of my strength back and I point to the kitchen. Sage, runs to the kitchen with his gun pointed to inspect things. He comes back to the foyer seconds later.

"Are you alright? What happened?" Sage compassionately inquires.

I answer weakly, "I think so. If you would have been five minutes longer, I'd probably be dead. I got home from work and out of nowhere some guy was in the house attacking me."

"Well, I'm thankful that didn't happen. Besides, nobody is going to ever put their hands on you again. I'm sorry that I wasn't here sooner to help you," Sage replies.

"It's not your fault and besides you saved me before the real attack took place. That guy was gonna rape me too," I report.

"I see your clothes ripped off. It has to be Kevin or Eric. You've never had any trouble in this neighborhood until the fiasco with those two started, so I'm sold on it being them," Sage remarks. "I damn sure didn't see this one coming."

"Yes, I agree with you on that. me. It has to be one of them. I'm sick that I couldn't tell which one it was. We have to call the police. This attack has to be documented, but first I need to get cleaned up. I feel dirty," I respond.

"I think you should get cleaned up and head to the hospital, but I hope you don't intend to tell the police that you think one of them did it because they'll laugh in your face. We still have no proof. We'll be lucky if they even go talk to them," Sage voices.

"I have to call them to report the attack and whoever it was did damage to my house and the insurance company has to be notified. I'll have to have a police report to file a claim," I explain. "I don't need to go to the hospital. I'm only a little sore."

Why is Sage always so opposed to me calling

the police? It seems like every time something transpires, he's against calling the cops. What's his deal? It doesn't really matter because I'm calling the cops. Sage gets the boys squared away while I jump in the shower. When I get out of the shower, I call the cops to file a report.

Twenty minutes later the cops arrive. The person conducting the investigation is Detective Mosely. Detective Mosely asks me a series of questions about what happened here tonight. I tell him exactly what happened. The detective notices finger prints on the floor where me and the intruder tussled. Detective Mosely motions an officer to lift the prints off the floor. Additionally, they get prints off the back door where the guy came in. They leave after about an hour after of collecting information and interviewing Sage and me. Sage thanks the police officers as he goes outside with them to their patrol cars. Sage sees the box of flowers as soon as he walks back in the house after the cops depart.

"I know I didn't send that, so let me guess... One of your former lovers sent you a gift to win you back over," Sage remarks.

"I'm sure they're from one of them. Check it out for yourself," I order.

Sage goes over to the box and pops the lid. He sees the dead flowers and is offended by them too. Again, he agrees with me that Eric and Kevin are playing games. They're clearly stating that they want me dead. Why else would they send me dead flowers?

"Is there a card or anything to identify where the flowers came from?" Sage asks.

"There is a card, but I didn't notice if there was a florist's name on it. I'll check," I answer.

I go to the card, but there's nothing identifying a florist on it. Sage opens the box again to see if there's anything mixed in with the dead flowers that can help. Fortunately, he finds a business card inside the box from the florist. I call the florist to see if they will tell me who paid for the flowers. The person who answered the phone tells me that the flowers were paid for by Kevin with his credit card. I get off the phone and tell Sage what the lady said.

"We got his ass now. The flowers came from the shop not too far from here and Kevin's dumb ass paid for them. Don't try to talk me out of it this time because I'm calling the cops back no matter what you say," I dictate.

Sage asserts, "Oh, I'm not stopping you this time. It makes sense that you call them back because his name is attached to those flowers. Now, we can give the cops something concrete to go on. The authorities need to deal with him."

"Thank you, for being on my side this time. I'll call them back after I put the boys to bed," I utter.

"I'm always on your side even though you don't always see it. No, I'll take care of the boys.

You call the cops and handle that. By the time you finish with the cops, the boys will be asleep, and then you can get some rest," Sage orates. "I'll rub you down to help alleviate your soreness."

This is why I never stopped loving Sage. He supports me and makes me better. Sage takes the boys upstairs and reads them a story. I call the detective who was just at my house and he returns within minutes. The cop comes and I tell him about the dead flowers and where they came from. He tells me that he will contact the florist in an effort to verify what I told him. I knew I wasn't crazy for thinking it was Kevin or Eric harassing me.

CHAPTER 14
Kevin's Perspective

I'm relaxing on the couch with Leslie. We've really been spending a lot of time together. The way we initially came together is now just one crazy story. We both agree that it was fortuitous that we met. The sex we have is even better than our first encounter. She has a better understanding of what I like and vice versa. It doesn't matter that she's a few years younger than me because she's fun to be with, very articulate, intelligent, and beautiful. I can tell that she's going places and those are the type of people I like to associate with.

Unfortunately, our relaxing evening is interrupted by a pounding on my door. Who the hell is pounding on my door like they're the police?

"Who is it?" I ask angrily.

"It's the Washington D.C. Police. I'm officer Mosely. We need to speak with Kevin Richardson," the cop replies.

Oh shit! It is the police. What the hell do they want with me?

"One second. Me and my lady need to put some clothes on," I respond nervously.

My first thought is to make a run for it out the back door, but then I'd be on the run. That's no way to live. Sheena probably told the cops that I'm the one who burned the lounge down, but I'll never admit it. I guess it's time to face the music. I knew what I was doing was wrong and could have heavy consequences and I still chose to do it. There's no need in crying about it now. I look out the window and see two units outside and I slowly walk over to the door and open it.

I say, "Hello officers. I'm Kevin Richardson. How can I help you?"

"We had a complaint filed about you harassing a woman by the name of Sheena Mills. She's pretty upset about this whole situation and fears for her safety," Officer Mosely claims.

"I've done nothing to make her feel unsafe and I was attacked at her home by one of her friends, but I'm not complaining. Things got a little out of hand, but that was it. No hard feelings. I even sent her some flowers as a peace offering," I verbalize.

"That's actually what we came to talk to you about. We're glad you admit to sending those flowers. That's the problem and why she's startled. Those flowers were inappropriate and definitely threatening," says Officer Mosely. "They were hardly a peace offering."

"Officer, I'm confused. Those are Miss Mills' favorite flowers. They were never threatening to her in the past. Those flowers were meant to be an 'I'm sorry' gesture. I don't see how they became a threat," I explain.

Officer Mosely states, "Well, a dozen dead flowers can scare anyone. Sheena Mills saw them as a death threat and I can see how she came to that conclusion. You can't stand here and tell us that you don't think dead flowers aren't ominous."

"I agree officer. Dead flowers are very disturbing. I wouldn't take that lightly either. It seems like you're saying that I sent Sheena dead flowers, but I didn't. I never touched the flowers. The florist delivered them. If they delivered dead flowers, I know nothing of it. This is news to me. I want my money back. That dozen and delivery cost me over a hundred bucks," I explain.

"So, you're saying that you didn't deliver the flowers yourself?" Officer Mosely asks.

"Sir, that's exactly what I'm saying. You can call the florist yourself," I verbalize.

Officer Mosely calls the florist and confirms what I told him. The florist assures the officer that they didn't deliver a dozen of dead irises on my behalf. Furthermore, the florist asserts that their delivery person delivered a fresh dozen of irises to the residence in question. The officer apologizes for the disturbance and leaves. I tell him that it's no problem and to call me if any more questions arise.

Leslie is upset that the police even came to bother me about something so petty. She really doesn't like for our time to be interrupted by anyone or anything especially pertaining to Sheena. She hasn't quite gotten over Sheena and Ilesha roughing her up in the bathroom at the lounge. I don't blame her because I haven't gotten over Sage catching me off guard at the lounge either.

"Really? Some silly flowers? Why does she think that you're even studying her like that? Doesn't she know that you're done with her?" asks Leslie.

I reply, "Sheena looks for people to blame when things go wrong in her life. She can't accept fault for the things she does. I guess she wants me to be her scapegoat in this case, but I'm not the one. I only sent the flowers as a peace offering. I've moved on and I'm with you now."

Leslie conveys, "That's so childish. I mean she really needs to grow up. It's sad that she's older than me, but acts like a high school girl."

"I know right. Listen, I don't want to talk about her or any of that garbage. She's already managed to disrupt our quality time, so let's not allow her to intervene any further," I mention.

Leslie takes my advice and we drop the Sheena conversation. Instead, we watch a movie on Netflix and chill. After the movie ends, Leslie and I go upstairs and pleasure each other like we've done so many times now. A couple of hours later, Leslie goes home to get ready for tomorrow. I decide to catch some shuteye. I'll be in meetings all day tomorrow, so I need to be well rested. I don't want to doze off in the meetings.

Just as I'm falling asleep, my phone rings. I hate when I forget to turn my ringer off before I go to bed. I always have a hard time falling back asleep once I've been awakened. Who's calling me anyway? I look at the screen to see who it is and it's Eric. I know better than to answer his call now. If I do, we'll be on the phone all night plotting and scheming. I decide not to answer his call, so I can get some sleep. I send his call to voicemail, turn my ringer off, and go to sleep. I'll call him after work tomorrow.

Talk about a good night's rest! That was exactly what I needed. I'm wide awake and ready to tackle this all-day meeting. The meeting won't be too bad because I'm well rested and because it's going to be somewhat interactive. These types of meetings are far more enjoyable than the ones that you have to sit down the entire time. If I continue to feel the way I feel right now, I'll be the number one participant in the meeting.

The meeting is well underway and my phone

hasn't stopped vibrating. Eric is calling and texting nonstop, Leslie's texting me about her day, and Sheena has even called. I really don't know what to think about Sheena calling me. She's probably calling to fuss about those dead flowers that she thinks I sent. I have to admit that it was a good trick.

Since I'm more than eager to know what Sheena left on my voicemail, I head to the restroom to listen to it. It's what I suspected. Sheena is yelling and full of histrionic antics like always. She's cursing me out on a recording. I've always found it funny when people leave absurd messages on a recording. I don't listen to the entire message because I don't need to hear her nonsense. However, I am amused that she's so perturbed.

Back to the meeting I go. We are more than halfway through the meeting and I haven't yawned once. The rest of the day is smooth. We have to do a couple of group activities in the meeting. I am not mad at that because it really helps the time go by quickly. After the last presentation, we are cut loose for the day.

I part ways with my colleagues and go to my car. I text Leslie back and then I call Eric to see why he's been antagonizing my phone.

"What's up man? Is everything alright?" I inquire.

"Yeah, all is well. I want to meet to tell you how we can do this. I have it all figured out,"

Eric replies enthusiastically.

"Good, I was hoping you didn't want to talk over the phone because you never know who's listening. Well I just got off, so I'm free to meet now," I comment.

"Bet, I will meet you at the bar on Georgia Ave. in thirty minutes," Eric states.

"See you there," I say.

I make my way to the bar to meet Eric. I hope he has it all figured out like he said he does. Sheena and Sage disgust me. They're parading around town like they're Romeo and Juliet. It wasn't that long ago that she hated Sage and loved me. This shit has to end soon. No, it will end soon.

I walk in the bar and Eric is already here. We down a couple of beers while we chat. Eric is beyond excited about his plan.

"You're gonna love it. I'm telling you, man," Eric mentions.

I urge, "Well, spill the beans. Stop being so damn secretive."

"The alcohol. It's all in the alcohol," Eric words with such pride.

"What the hell is in the alcohol? Why are you speaking in tongue? Is that beer kicking your ass?" I ask.

"Listen, you know Sheena and her friends always drink whenever they get together, so all we have to do is put a little something in her bottles of alcohol and we're good to go. Sheena and

Sage will drink the stuff and fall out dead. The beauty is that we'll be nowhere near there when it happens," Eric explains.

I remark, "That's not as good of a plan as I thought you would have. You don't have any way to get to the liquor. It's not like she'll just give you the bottles to poison them."

"I know that, fool. I'll sneak into her house and put the poison in the bottles myself. No problem," Eric shoots back.

"And how do you plan to get into the house? You do know Sheena changed all the locks?" I ask.

"I have unrestricted access through the garage. One day I snuck into her garage after she pulled in. I purchased a universal garage door opener and programmed it to her garage door. I can get in with no problem now," Eric reports.

"Oh, that's great! I see you've been planning ahead," I voice.

"Yeah, I'm quite the brain. I have to admit it," Eric speaks confidently.

"Shit!!! There's a problem with that too. The garage door is broken. You won't be able to gain access that way," I mention.

"How do you know that?" asks Eric.

I answer, "I know because I damaged the door one night. I figured it would be easier to get Sheena walking up the steps than through the garage."

"Damn! I can see your thinking on that. It

makes sense, but we need the door fixed. Access through the garage is paramount. We have to have it. I was wondering why Sheena went through the front door the other day when I was scoping her place out. I figured she saw the box of flowers and went through the front for that reason," Eric states.

"Well, we have to wait until she gets the door fixed," I say. "By the way, that was a nice move you made by switching the flowers out with dead ones! That dumb ass cop thought he had me."

"Thanks man. Do you think you can undo whatever you did to damage it?" Eric asks.

I respond, "I don't know. I pushed it in to bend it off the track. It shouldn't take much to fix it. I'll see what I can do, but it's risky to even go back over there."

"Gotcha, I don't think you should risk going back over there just for the door. You won't know if it's fixed anyway," Eric verbalizes.

"Right, I know Sheena won't let that door stay broken for too long. She'll get Sage to fix it or call a serviceman out to get it straight. We just have to be ready," I utter.

We have the details of the plan worked out. We part ways and I head home. Leslie is waiting for me to get there, so we can eat dinner. My baby cooked for me tonight. I go home, eat dinner, and chat with Leslie before going to bed.

The next day, I drive past Sheena's house to see if there's been any change in the garage door situation. While driving past, I observe that the garage door is fully open. Sage is in the driveway while a man in a uniform is doing something to the door. He's fixing the door. Eric and I can proceed with our plan.

I call Eric on the way home and inform him of the fixed garage door. He is glad about the news of the door and is ready to sneak into Sheena's house tomorrow. We have to be at Sheena's house early, so he can get into the house.

"How do you know tomorrow is an ideal time to drop the poison? You don't think we need to know when they will be drinking it?" I ask.

Eric answers, "Of course we need to know when they'll most likely be drinking and we do."

Eric pulls out his phone and opens up Facebook. Sage put up a post that stated he's making dinner tomorrow night. They'll be drinking for sure.

The next morning Sage leaves with the boys like clockwork. Next, Sheena backs out of the garage and drives away. I pull out of the parking space we are in and drop Eric off. He hits the garage door button and the door begins to open. He slips under the door and closes it behind him.

I pull away and park several blocks down the street to wait for Eric. About ten minutes later he calls me to come pick him up. I pull back up in front of the house, he jumps in, and we quickly disappear without being seen. Now, all we have to do is wait. The trap has been set.

CHAPTER 15
Sheena's Perspective

I need to call my girls. I've been busy to say the least and haven't talked to them much. We've only sent a few texts back and forth, but no phone calls. I know they're going to get on me for being out of the loop, but I'll make up for it when I invite them over for dinner. I call Rachel first.

"Hey, girl. I'm so glad you answered. Feel like we haven't talked in months," I say.

Rachel replies, "Hi, honey. Yes, it's been too long. You are keeping my boys from me. I need to see them. I have some things for them too."

"I know I've been busy with all that's going on. The boys definitely miss you. In fact, you should come over tonight for dinner. I'm not gonna lie; it was Sage's idea. He wants to formally apologize to you, Ilesha, and me for all he's put us through. He's cooking dinner," I report.

"That's very nice of him. A formal apology is a noble gesture. I can make it over tonight for dinner. Besides, I want to see the boys badly," Rachel comments.

"Great! Dinner will be ready by seven, so any time around then is perfect to come by," I voice.

Rachel lets me know that she'll be over well before 7, so she can get some time in with the boys. Next, I call Ilesha. I don't know how she's going to take the news of Sage inviting her to dinner, but I'll throw it at her anyway. She's not as forgiving and accepting as Rachel. I won't blame her if she doesn't want to come to dinner. She has a right not to come and I'll love her no matter what she decides.

"Hey, girl," I say as she answers the phone.

"Bitch, don't hey girl me. You know you need to start with an apology for not calling me lately. You back to salivating over Sage, so you don't know how to call anymore," Ilesha states.

"Now, you know that's not the case. I've been busy as hell and you haven't called me either. Now, that's like the pot calling the kettle black," I shoot back.

Ilesha responds, "Don't do me. The radio station has had me busier than three hells. Hell, I just got back to town about three hours ago."

"Trust me, I know all about it. The boys

really miss you and I do too," I mention.

"Aww, I know they do. I miss them too, but I don't miss your ass. It's good to have a break from your needy ass. Hell, you needed us so much that I started to move in with you. I woulda saved a lot of gas money," Ilesha informs.

"Ilesha, girl you know you got a few screws loose. Well, if you miss the boys so much you should come over for dinner tonight. Rachel already said she's coming," I verbalize.

"Girl, that sounds good! I just had a light snack, but I'm looking for a home cooked meal. I really didn't feel like cooking tonight. All I've eaten over the last few days is restaurant food. Just let me know what time and I'll be there," Ilesha utters.

"Okay girl, but there's one thing with dinner. Sage is cooking it. He wants to apologize formally for the things he did to us," I word.

"Shit, now I don't know about that. I don't know if I can keep from slapping the shit outta him. You know how I get," Ilesha speaks.

"Girl, I need you to do this for me. I don't want you to love him, but he's the boys' father and you are my sister. I would like for this to be as peaceful of a union as possible," I remark.

Ilesha voices, "I'll do it for you and the boys. However, I'm not doing it for Sage. I hope he doesn't think his flattery and charm will win me over. I'll be reading his ass for insincerity the entire night."

I thank her for her willingness to try to make it work. I know she'll be scoping Sage's every movement and analyzing his every utterance. We end the call and I go run some errands. While running errands, I text Sage to let him know that Rachel and Ilesha will be joining us for dinner. Sage is excited about their willingness to allow him to make things right. We hang up and I go to get my eyebrows done. While I'm waiting to get my eyebrows done, I notice that Sage posted a comment on Facebook about cooking dinner for us. He's clearly hyped about tonight. I continue with the happenings of my day.

Around five o'clock I make it back to my house to meet Sage. Since the attack, he's been staying with me. He doesn't want me and the boys to ever be in a precarious situation like that again. It really troubled him that he wasn't there to protect me and he swore that would never happen again. Moments later, Sage pulls up with the boys and we go inside. He makes a beeline to the kitchen, so he can do his thing. I take the boys upstairs to their room because Sage wants dinner to be a surprise. I don't know why his meal is such a secret, but it is. How can somebody put me out of my own kitchen?

Rachel shows up about forty five minutes later. I open the door and greet her with a long embrace as if I haven't seen her in years. She comments on how good the food smells and attempts to go to the kitchen to see what's cooking. I step in front of her to slow her progress.

"Honey, what's wrong? Is something wrong in the kitchen?" Rachel asks.

"Yes, something is wrong. Sage is wrong," I answer jokingly. "He won't allow me to be in my own kitchen."

"That's so sweet! He wants it to be a huge surprise. You can't blame him for being a sweetie pie. You have to admire a man who knows his way around the kitchen," Rachel states.

"I guess. I just think he's a control freak," I say.

"Well, all men have a touch of control freak in them. He's just being a man. I hope he doesn't think I'm being rude by not speaking to him. I'll blame you for not allowing me into the kitchen," Rachel comments.

I assure her that we don't need to worry about Sage, but I'll take the blame if need be. We laugh at the conversation as we walk upstairs. Rachel goes to the boys' room and plays with them. She also gives them the gifts she brought for them.

"Ooh, girl those outfits are gonna be so cute on them! They will look like little gentlemen. Now, that's what I'm talking about. I would say that those outfits were expensive, but I know you better than that," I comment.

"You know I found a great deal on those outfits. You know I always save a penny when I can," Rachel asserts.

We talk a little more about the boys and then the doorbell rings. I peek out the window and see Ilesha's car. By the time I make it downstairs, Sage has made it to the door. Ilesha is shocked by Sage opening the door and there's a short stare down between the two of them. I don't know if Ilesha is going to swing at him, cut him, or what.

"Hi, Ilesha," Sage utters.

"Sage," Ilesha replies curtly as she rolls her eyes.

"Hey, girl. I shoulda known you were gonna come over looking like you're going to a fashion show. It is just dinner," I say.

"Bitch, you know I don't come out the house looking any type of way. That's just not how I do. It doesn't matter that it's just dinner," Ilesha reminds.

"I know, but damn. Well, the boys are looking for you upstairs. Rachel's up there with them," I tell.

Sage goes back to the kitchen after Ilesha greets him coldly. Ilesha and I go upstairs with Rachel and the boys. Ilesha doesn't say anything in front of Sage, but she comments to us how great the food smells. She's going to play hardball with Sage no matter what. A little while later, Sage calls us downstairs because dinner is almost ready. The kitchen smells great and is beautifully adorned. He bought all new place mats and silverware for dinner. Sage always goes overboard.

Sage has made the amount of food that's commensurate with Thanksgiving dinner. He has prepared a variety of dishes. There's grilled lemon pepper chicken, crab legs, lobster, and homemade biscuits just to name a few items. Rachel and I are thoroughly impressed and so is Ilesha, but she doesn't let Sage know. Before we eat, Sage makes an announcement.

"I'm thankful that all of you showed up tonight. I know we've all traveled a very long road to end up here together today. It's funny how these are the same people in this room who were present when I first bumped into Sheena at In the Mix. Minus the boys of course. I want to take this opportunity to apologize to you sisters for what my actions could have done to your friendship. I mean this from the bottom of my heart," Sage orates.

"We all have our flaws. I forgive you Sage. The Lord wanted me to forgive, so I have," says Rachel.

"Thank you. I know everyone in this room may not forgive me as quickly and I understand that. I'll right that ship in time through my words and actions. Let it be known that I couldn't be more proud to have fathered two perfect children. Furthermore, I'm honored to have you, Sheena Mills, as the mother of my children. You are the only woman I've ever romantically loved," Sage vocalizes.

"I agree with you on that. The boys are perfect," Ilesha butts in.

"Of course they're perfect because I gave birth to them," Sheena jokes.

We all laugh as I high five Rachel. The mood is very sentimental as Sage speaks, so I decide to enter a little levity. Ilesha tells me that she is the only one with premium pussy in the room. Rachel tells Ilesha to watch her mouth around the boys. Ilesha apologizes to the boys and me and we continue on.

Sage states, "A different man stands before you today. Like I said, I'm honored to have you as the mother of my children and I thank God daily that it's you. You - the woman I love, the only woman I've ever loved, and the only woman I will ever love. I never wanted to have children out of wedlock, but that's the situation we are faced with today. I hope to change that very soon."

Sage walks over to me and grabs my hand. Next, he leads me a few feet away from the table and directly in front of the boys. Rachel senses what's going on and pulls out her phone and starts recording. Sage reaches in his back pocket and takes out a handkerchief. He slowly unfolds the handkerchief until a ring is revealed. Sage drops down on both knees. I don't know if he's really going to beg or if he doesn't know that one knee would have been fine.

"Miss, let's do this the right way. Let's raise

our kids under the union of marriage. I want us to spend holidays together the way it's meant to be," Sage states.

"Sage, you are gonna make me cry," I say as tears form in my eyes.

"Sheena, you are who I want to make happy forever and who I want to give a good morning kiss to every morning. I want you to be my wife," Sage communicates.

"Sage, what are you saying?" I ask.

"It's not what I'm saying. It's what I'm asking. Sheena, will you marry me?" Sage asks.

I look at my girls in utter shock. I have my free hand over my mouth because I am totally astonished. I never expected this to happen period. I didn't see that Sage was really planning an engagement party for me. I'm almost losing my breath because the man of my dreams just asked for my hand in marriage. Tears are forming in the corner of my eyes because I'm so happy. My girls are looking at me to see what I'm going to say. I decide not to let them wait for my response any longer.

"Yes, I will marry you," I respond in a cracking voice.

Sage places a ring on my finger that's the size of an ice cube. We kiss and then embrace in a very special and magical moment. Sage wipes a tear from my eye as it trickles down my cheek. I can't help but think how right this feels. I know this is right. I let Sage go and then turn to my boys and hug and kiss them. Rachel and Ilesha get up from the table and we enjoy a sisterly hug. They congratulate me on my engagement. Rachel congratulates Sage too. Ilesha doesn't quite congratulate Sage.

"Sage, you did good tonight, but listen if you hurt my sister again, I'm gonna hurt you," Ilesha warns.

"Well, this is definitely a celebration! Please tell me that you have purchased some champagne for this joyous occasion," comments Rachel.

Sage grabs the champagne that he has on ice. We all toast to the success of our future union. We continue eating and telling old stories. In our own way, we are like a family that has made it through the storm. I'm happy and I know my boys will be in the future. They'll never know that their mommy almost had two baby daddies. I know I won't tell them.

"Okay, the champagne is good, but I want an amaretto sour. You know that's my drink of choice," I convey.

"You relax with your girls. I'll fix it for you and I'll even go heavy on the cherries. I know how you like it. I already have some cherries soaking in the amaretto," Sage verbalizes.

"Girls, do you want one?" I ask.

Both Rachel and Ilesha decline the amaretto sours and enjoy the expensive champagne Sage has purchased. They also don't want to mix the two alcoholic beverages knowing they have to drive home. I should've known that Rachel wasn't going to have more than a few sips of the champagne tonight.

"Sage, are you gonna have a amaretto with me?" I inquire.

Sage answers, "No, I don't want any of that girly drink. I'm fine with the champagne. Besides, I have a lot of stuff to do, so I wanna be able to function properly."

"You are being a party pooper! Well, I'll enjoy one for all of you. It's my engagement and I'm turning up tonight," I remark.

"I'm perfectly fine with being a party pooper. I have no problem with that. Before I fix your drink, I have one more thing to give you," Sage words.

"Well, we all know that I like surprises. You really didn't have to. I mean this rock is enough," I reply.

"I know I didn't, but I want to give you something else. It's upstairs in your room. You should go get it," Sage verbalizes.

I zoom upstairs to find my gift. I look around for a few seconds, but I don't spot a present immediately. Sage is pulling my leg. I'm going to kill him for playing me like this. I decide to check my closet just in case my gift is in here. I inspect my closet and again I don't see a gift. When I exit my closet to go downstairs, Sage is in my bedroom and has closed the door behind him.

Sage has a very intent look in his eyes. He

walks over to me and grabs me by my neck and pushes me up against the wall. With my back to the wall, Sage kisses me wildly. It's like lust has overtaken his body. I kiss him back just as aggressively. Sage pulls my little black dress up just over my ass and begins tugging at my thong. Almost instantly, my thong is off and thrown to the other side of the room.

I undo Sage's belt buckle and quickly have his pants off of him. I pull his boxers partially down and then with my foot I wiggle his underwear down to his ankles. I place my foot on top of them as they're on the floor and motion Sage to step completely free of them. Now, we are free and clear to fuck.

"Wait, my girls are going to hear us. We need to stop. We can't fuck with them in the house," I verbalize.

"Fuck it! Let them hear us. You look exquisite tonight and I want to feel you now. I can't leave you alone. You got me feenin for you! I don't want to wait," Sage states.

"Well then, fuck me like only you know how," I order.

Sage bends me over doggie style at the edge of the bed. He slowly inserts half of his caramel rod into my pussy. I tense up and arch my back to brace for impact. Sage takes his hand and attempts to flatten my back. I know doggie style is his favorite position, so he's about to go haywire back there

"Loosen up Sheena. I'm gonna take care of your every sexual fantasy tonight. Don't be tense. There's no need to be," Sage says in his bedroom voice.

I follow his instructions and loosen up. I drop the arch in my back, bury my face in a pillow, and allow Sage to invade my body the way he desires. He passionately and sensually strokes my pussy in and out over and over. Sage subtly caresses my body. He runs his hand gently down my back as he continues to stroke.

He stares at my derriere and gently smacks and grabs it. As he prods my treasure chest, he takes his free hand and slides it up my back until he reaches my neck. He grabs my neck, not the back of my neck, but the front. Sage applies the perfect amount of pressure to my neck as he chokes and strokes me.

I moan and groan as Sage invades my walls like he's a Trojan soldier. I want to feel all of his dick inside of me, but he's only serving me half. I push back on his dick in an attempt to feel all ten inches, but Sage blocks me. Sage isn't fucking me fast, but I'm enjoying every stroke of his magic stick.

Sage grunts while I moan. He stops choking me and reaches under me and fondles my clit. I love when a man slow grinds my sweet spot while playing with my clit. I feel my body begin to get hot and my toes and fingers begin to tingle, so I know a great release is near. Sage leans forward, gently grabs my neck with his free hand and raises me up to where his mouth is by my ear.

He whispers, "I love you. Don't ever stop giving me this sweet pussy."

In the same marginally raised position, he keeps slowly sexing me. Our bodies are locked in. His chest is on my back and I can feel every beat of his heart. It's almost like our hearts are beating as one. That's how it used to be when we first started dating. Since Sage slightly raised my position, I feel more sensation to my clit.

I rub my nipples as Sage continues to dominate my walls. Now, Sage serves me the full ten inches and speeds up his strokes. I feel my pussy begin to gush with moisture and my nipples are getting hard. I'm about to blow. Sage is choking me, rubbing my clit, and subtly nibbling and kissing my collar bone simultaneously.

"Baby, don't stop. Please don't stop," I scream as I close my eyes and enjoy every moment.

My body convulses harder than it has in quite some time. I'm shaking violently to the point of being embarrassed. Sage keeps pumping my pussy and rubbing my clit. Just when I think I'm done, my body begins to erupt again. I'm having another orgasm.

After the third orgasm, I fall lifelessly on my stomach onto the bed. I'm sweating heavily and I can't catch my breath. Sage climbs on the bed and rests beside me. We cuddle as Sage jokes on me for cumming so hard. That was amazing. I really needed that. Sage hasn't gotten a nut, so I know I have to get him straight, but I can't move right now. Hell, I don't know when I'll be able to move again.

He's clearly still horny because he takes his heavy brown dick and smacks me on my ass with it. All I hear is "SMACK" on my ass as Sage laughs. I jump up with sudden heroism and grab Sage's scepter. It's heavy and veined up in need of some attention. I grab his dick and hold it to my face, but don't do anything to it initially.

After a few seconds, I can tell Sage is confused. I just let his dick fall on my face. As his dick rests on my face, I lick and suck his balls. I take one hand and begin beating his dick on my face. He loves it and so does my inner freak. I decide to do my hummer move on him to really blow his mind. I fondle is balls sensually and then place one of them in my mouth. Sage sighs and then I place his other ball in my mouth. I suck both of his testicles with just enough pressure to make it feel good. Next, I begin to hum as his balls are in my mouth. The vibration on his balls feels so good that his legs begin to wobble and he attempts to make me stop. Eventually, he pulls away from me enough to pop his nuts out of my mouth. I have him wide open now and begin beating his dick on my face again as I look up into his eyes.

I stop beating his dick on my face and suck

it. Sage massages the back of my head while I pleasure him. I move my tongue skillfully all around his dick and balls. As I pull my mouth off of his dick, there is a stream of pre-cum leading to my mouth. Without hesitation, I begin sucking it again. He loves it and is squirming on the bed.

"Ooh, ahh," Sage lets out.

I spit on his dick and keep serving him. I attempt to put the entire ten inches in my mouth, but I begin to gag on it before I accomplish my goal. Sage's dick is a steel beam and it's time for my hot pussy to melt it down. I mount Sage as he lies flat on his back.

I slowly move my body like a snake as I twirl around on his cane. Sage grabs my hips as I bounce up and down on his dick. I reach down and massage Sage's balls while he gropes my tits. His dick gets harder inside of me. Sage pulls me close to him and begins sucking my breasts while we fuck. Sweat is running down my back between my ass cheeks. Each time I wind my pussy down Sage's bar, I splash him with sweat, but he doesn't flinch. Instead, it turns him on. He speeds up with every sweat bead and moan I provide.

My curls have flattened, my hair is sweaty, and is sticking to my face. I wipe my hair out of my face, but it's to no avail because it goes right back. I pull my legs from under me and now I'm in a squatting position over Sage. I grab Sage around his neck in order to brace myself a little and then I pounce up and down violently on his elongated cock. The bed is creaking profusely. I'm bouncing on him like he's a trampoline. Two of my pictures fall off of my night stand from the force of me pouncing on his dick. Every time I land on his rock I feel a paralyzing blow to my spine, but I don't stop.

The bed is banging the wall and the bed is even jumping off the floor with every reentry. The smell of fucking engrosses the air. We are in the moment. The mattress begins to slide while we fuck, but we don't stop to adjust it.

"You wanna fuck, I see. Then fuck me then," Sage orders.

All I hear is the sound of my pussy being penetrated nonstop, the bed banging the wall, and the sound of my ass bouncing off of Sage's dick. The mattress slides so far to the left that we eventually fall off of the bed, but we keep fucking. Nothing is going to stop us now. I'm rubbing my clit while we're on the floor fucking and I cum again. To my surprise, Sage manages to stand while I'm still riding him.

He keeps me airborne and puts his back against the wall. Sage has a firm grip on my ass while I ride him. I'm sure his hands are leaving an imprint in my ass cheeks. We are face to face and eye to eye in our sexual encounter. He's trying to outdo me and I him. Who will win? Sage kisses me and I slow down my body to the speed of our kissing. My juices are pouring out of me. They are flowing down his dick onto his balls. I have never been this wet. EVER!! His dick feels so good that I want to cry. This is euphoria and I never want to leave.

Before I know it, Sage whisks me to the dresser and places me on it. He spreads my legs apart and stoops down a little bit. I feel his warm and wet tongue whirling on my clit. I breathe deeply and lean back against the mirror as he tastes me. I grab his head and motion it circularly. He puts two fingers in my pussy and continues licking my clit.

I rock my body back and forth to slow grind on his fingers. "Slurp" is all I hear as my pussy overflows with secretions. His tongue is amazing. Sage really has stepped his sexual abilities up, since our last dealings. He seems to be more in tune with pleasing me than getting a nut for himself.

Sage stops eating my pussy and yanks me forward. I'm now closer to being flat on my back. Sage completely stretches one of my legs as if forcing me into a full split which really spreads me wide open. He has equal access to my pussy and ass. He licks my ass like he's licking the cake bowl.

As I'm enjoying my ass eating, I play with my nipples and fondle myself. My whole body tingles and my clit begins to get hard. I'm panting and squirming out of control. I start cumming again. While I'm getting off, Sage inserts his entire dick into my pussy and begins pounding.

Sage must know that I need a good pounding to complete this session. I've released countless times, so now I want to fuck. I feel his dick punching through my walls. Sage grips me by my ass and pulls me toward him while he stuffs his rod inside of me. Sage is fucking me with no regard for noise or anything. The dresser is rocking back and forth violently.

Sage stops for a second and repositions me. My back is up against the mirror and Sage resumes fucking me. My walls are stretched open as I scream Sage's name.

"You like that?" Sage asks.

"No, I love it," I say seductively.

Sage asks, "Whose pussy it?"

I answer, "It's yours daddy. This pussy is all yours."

"Damn right it is!" Sage asserts.

The dirty talk clearly incites Sage because he goes to another level of penetration. The dresser is hitting the wall and rocking back and forth so much that it's about to tip over. My pussy is flowing like raging rapids.

"Yeah, baby. I'm almost there. This pussy feels so damn good," Sage comments.

Seconds later my pussy starts contracting again as I cum. My pussy grabs Sage's dick with every convulsive action my it does. Sage begins to cum at the same time as I do. He speeds up and releases a manly grunt as he cums. The strokes Sage gives me are so deep, swift, and hard that the mirror hits the wall too hard and breaks free of the dresser. Sage gets the last strokes of his nut out and staggers back as his cum and my juices drip from his dick. I can't move. My energy has been sapped from my body. All I can do is breathe heavily and lie on top of the dresser in disbelief of how I just got fucked. Sage has never looked more handsome to me in my life as his sweaty, naked, and chiseled body stands before me.

I know my girls heard every second of our impromptu fuck session. I know they'll tease me nonstop the first chance they get. I get cleaned up, pull my hair up, and go back downstairs. My entire body is like one giant noodle. I'm no good for anything at this moment.

My girls, the boys, and I move to the living room and converse. Moments later, Sage makes it back downstairs. Sage brings me my drink and goes back to clean up the kitchen. The girls find it comical that he's washing the dishes. They say that most men run away from the kitchen when it's time to wash the dishes. I don't find it strange because all of my former men cooked and cleaned for me. I guess I'm just special. Rachel sends the video of the proposal to Sage, Ilesha, and me. We all upload the video to our social media accounts. I know I'm going to be the envy of the town when the ladies see my huge rock.

"And just so you know… Bitch, you nasty as hell!" Ilesha states.

Rachel comments, "Yes, and brazen too. You two didn't even try to handle your business discreetly. With all of that noise you two were making, I almost left."

"I'm sorry ladies, but you know how it is when you get caught in the moment. One minute you're talking and the next thing you know you're airborne getting fucked," I reply.

"That's happened to me several times. Start out talking and then have a dick in my mouth," admits Ilesha.

We laugh as we chat and I sip on my amaretto sour. I love my sisters to death.

CHAPTER 16
Kevin's Perspective

"They've been in there for hours. Do you think they've drunk the alcohol?" asks Eric.

"They've definitely had some drinks by now. You know how they like to drink," I reply.

Eric states, "Well, they should all be dead by now. That stuff I put in the liquor bottles is toxic. I'm about to go in the house."

I explain, "You can't go in there just yet. If for some reason they're still alive, you'll be finished."

"I know, but at some point I have to go in the house to get the liquor bottles. If they're all in there dead from poisoning, you know the police will eventually test the bottles, so I have to get them. I have to pour them out and replace them with uncontaminated bottles," Eric comments. "Not to mention that I have to check on the boys. We can't just leave them unattended for hours."

"Alright, I see your point. I'll wait here and be the lookout. If something doesn't look right, I'll call you, so be mindful of your phone," I convey.

Eric gets out of the car after assuring me he'll be mindful of his phone. He heads towards Sheena's house like a thief in the night. I'm on the lookout while surfing the internet. I open my Facebook account and see that a video has been shared.

I watch the video and it's a video of Sheena and Sage getting engaged. I don't think that they're in the house dead at all. They're celebrating a damn engagement. There's no way Sheena had me burn the lounge down and now she's engaged to Sage. Damn, Eric can't open that garage door right now. They'll hear him for sure.

I call Eric immediately in an attempt to keep him from opening the garage door. That'll be totally unexplainable. Pick up the phone damn it! Pick up the damn phone! My calls go unanswered, so I jump out of the car and head down the street to Sheena's.

I'm trying to think of an excuse as to why we would have access to the garage door just in case Eric gets caught. What can I say? He must be inside the garage by now if he hasn't called or texted back. Maybe they are dead. I'm sure they had drinks during dinner and after the proposal. That's just a normalcy for a celebration.

I make it over to the house and I initially don't see Eric. I call his name in a whisper and Eric responds. He's ducked down between the cars in the driveway. I duck down in between the cars with him and tell him about the engagement video. He's dumbfounded and a little unfocused.

We get up and run back to the car in order to regroup. I show him the video and he's enraged just as I am. Clearly, the alcohol poisoning didn't work.

"Fuck, fuck, fuck! The poison didn't work, but I know how to handle this. It ends tonight," Eric verbalizes.

"How so? What do you have in mind?" I inquire.

"You don't want to know. Just leave now and go somewhere with a lot of people, so you'll have an alibi," Eric orders.

"Eric, what are you going to do?" I ask.

Eric flashes his gun to me and turns to get out of the car. I grab him by the arm in an attempt to keep him from doing what he has on his mind. He has the look of a lover scorned. He yanks away from me and exits the car.

I chase him down the street back to our former hiding spot. Eric is possessed with revenge and isn't backing down. This is totally not the plan for the night. Hell, I'm always on board with monitoring and adjusting, but this is ridiculous.

"Why did you follow me?" Eric asks in a low

voice.

"I followed you to stop you from doing this dumb shit. This wasn't the plan. It was supposed to be cleanly done and this is hardly that," I assert.

"Well, I'm to the point of no return. I've tried to be nice, but that didn't work. I've tried to plan it out and that's not working. I'm at my wit's end. This time I'm going haywire, so you better get outta here. You don't have to go down with me," Eric vocalizes.

"Come on man, there has to be another way. Let's rethink this thing," I offer.

"No more rethinking. No more being nice. I'm going to open this garage door and the first person I see is getting shot and then I'll continue shooting until they're all dead," Eric dictates.

"I implore you to reconsider, but I won't fight you. I'm outta here," I say.

As soon as I make a motion to stand, the garage door begins to open. Is it possible that we've been detected? We both run to the side of the house under the cloak of darkness. Seconds later, Sage appears carrying Sheena out of the garage and places her in the car. Rachel and Ilesha follow right behind carrying some of Sheena's belongings and the boys.

Eric whispers, "Even better. I'm gonna unload on them right now. It'll look totally random."

"Hell no you won't. You could easily shoot

the boys if you miss. I don't know about you, but I can't live with that on my conscious. Now, isn't the time," I communicate.

Eric weighs what I said. He decides to chill for a second to see what's going on with them. Obviously, something is wrong with Sheena, but what? Is she sick from the alcohol? If she is sick from the poison, why aren't the others sick? We listen to what's going on.

Rachel states, "I hope Sheena's going to be okay."

"I told her ass not to mix the champagne with the amaretto, but she didn't listen. That's why I didn't drink any of it," Ilesha remarks.

"Yeah, seems like a bad decision now. Honestly, she seems a little sicker than a little mixed liquor," Sage says.

"Well, let's be glad that we all didn't mix the drinks. I still think we should have called 911 for her," Rachel voices.

"Hell no girl. This is D.C. By the time they'd show up, we'd already be at the hospital," remarks Ilesha.

"Okay, well I'm taking the boys home with me. They don't need to be exposed to any germs in the hospital. I'm going home to get some clothes for tomorrow and then I'm coming right back here. Ilesha, let me know something as soon as you know," Rachel says.

They leave the house. Eric and I wait for them to get a few minutes away. Eric hits the garage door button and the door lifts. We leave our hiding spot on the side of the house and enter the garage. Sheena's been poisoned and the evidence is still in the house. We have to retrieve the evidence just in case. We ease back into Sheena's house and switch the bottles in an effort to remove any evidence from the house. We make the switch and leave Sheena's place without incident.

Leslie calls me as soon as I walk through my front door. I'm glad she called because I need some company after the crazy night I've had. She tells me that she's free to stop by tonight. Leslie comes over in an outfit that rivals her Halloween costume. Obviously, she loves dressing up because she's wearing a French Maid costume. We get straight to having sex. It's a real fuck fest. She knows just how to give it to me. She's allowing me to get rid of all of this aggression I have inside. After our session, we relax in bed.

"Damn, you must've really needed to get off. You were an animal and I loved it," Leslie states.

"Yeah, I really did. I'm glad you came over. Damn, you know you give what I need when I need it," I respond.

We continue talking while we chill in bed. Leslie falls asleep, so I surf the web and wait to see what's going on with Sheena. Someone shared a post that states that she's going to be alright. Sheena apparently had to get her stomach pumped at the hospital. Damn, I have to call

Eric to let him know.

"Eric, we have a problem. Your girl is gonna be alright and of course nobody else even got sick. We missed them," I inform.

"I know bro. I saw it on Facebook. Saw a post that said they'll be cutting her loose soon. It's over man," Eric speaks.

"It's not over because we know exactly where they'll be. They have to take Sheena back home, so we can just meet them there and do what we have to do. There is no way she's marrying that bastard Sage and pinning the club getting burned down on me. No fucking way," I orate.

"It's like you said before, there's no way we can get away with it if we both go. It's definitely a two man job because it's going to be at least four of them. It's too many people to account for to do alone. If we go with just us two, we'll have no alibi and the police will surely come for us," Eric reports.

"I thought about that. We just have to use technology in our favor. These investigators love to check cell phone towers to see where people last used their phones, so we'll make sure we don't have them with us," I comment.

Eric remarks, "That's not enough to get us off the hook because they'll see that there was no cellular activity on either one of our phones."

"That's where you're wrong. My phone has a feature where I can program it to send text messages at whatever time I want. I'm sure yours does too. I'll program it to text you at a certain time and then you set yours to text me back. We'll choreograph the messages to seem like we're conversing through text," I explain.

Eric words, "I get it! The cell towers pick up our cell phones as being nowhere near there and we're in the clear. Now, that's slick!"

"Exactly! Well, we need to get moving now if we're going to get back to Sheena's house in time to do our thing. We have to make another quick pit stop if we're really going to make our story believable," I say.

Eric inquires, "A pit stop? Where do you have in mind?"

"Listen, meet me at the bar in DuPont Circle. We'll go in there and order a couple of double shots of tequila, but not really drink them. After a few, we can act like we've had too much to drink and then we leave. Once we leave the bar in our cars, you can park your car and jump in with me and we'll head to Sheena's house to finally settle this thing. After that, I'll take you back to your car and we'll be in the clear," I verbalize.

"When does our fake text message conversation come into play?" Eric asks.

"I got you. It comes into play once we leave the bar. I'll leave my phone around the corner from the bar in some bushes and you leave yours in the car," I answer. "I'll explain the rest at the bar when I see you."

"Alright, I'm leaving for the bar now," Eric states.

Next, I wake Leslie up and tell her that I really need to make an important move and she's free to stay here for the rest of the night. She's a little upset that I'm bouncing on her, but she understands that I have to handle my business. It's my house. I drive to the bar to meet Eric. When I arrive at the bar, Eric is already inside and has ordered two double shots. We actually drink the first round of double shots just to have alcohol on our breaths and in our systems.

Fortunately, Eric's phone has the same feature as mine that allows for his phone to send scheduled text messages. Eric and I plan out our fake conversation. While we scheme, we order two more rounds of double shots of tequila and then we leave the bar to head to Sheena's. We decide that in our bullshit text conversation that we're going to act like we had too much to drink at the bar and shortly after leaving the bar we pulled over to wait for the impact of the liquor to subside.

It's perfect because while we're at Sheena's place wreaking havoc, our phones will prove that we're on the other side of town in our cars half drunk. If the police check, the bartender will have to testify that we were there and had plenty of drinks. Between the phones' cell tower information and the bartender, we'll be in the clear if any investigation comes our way.

Eric and I leave the bar in our cars. We get two blocks from the bar and I slow down when I see a nicely sized bush. I roll down my window and toss my phone into the bushes. Eric follows me until we find a place for him to park his car. Finally, we find a spot for Eric to park his car and he jumps in with me. We drive to Sheena's house and park down the street. I have my gun and an extra two magazines and Eric has his gun along with the garage door opener. We jump out and zoom up to Sheena's place. Eric hits the fob to open the garage door and we go in. It's great that we beat them back because now we will really have the element of surprise on our side.

"Kevin, now that I think about it, we should probably wait in the house. We'll be able make sure the boys are tucked safely in their rooms before we attack," Eric suggests.

"I agree. We'll have more options being inside the house anyway. Hell, we know at some point that they'll all be inside the house, so it just makes sense for us to be inside too. We'll even have more places to hide in there," I convey.

We hear what sounds like a car pulling into the driveway. It's probably Rachel, but for all we know it could be Sage, Sheena, and Ilesha returning from the hospital. Eric and I scurry towards the door that leads into the house. Fortunately, I fumble my gun and pause to fully grab it. Eric goes through the door and is met by several rounds of gun fire. He gets shot several times. I'm glad he was in front of me because I would have been hit. I fire back several shots as I run through the door and take cover. Eric is on the floor motionless. He's dead for sure. What the hell is going on?

CHAPTER 17
Sage's Perspective

"Throw your gun down and I'll spare your life!" I shout.

Kevin replies as he shoots his gun without even coming close to hitting me, "Fuck you. I'm not throwing down shit. You can kiss my ass. The way I see it, you're the next one who will lose his life tonight."

"The way I see it, your plan is already blown to shambles. You didn't expect for me to be here. You definitely didn't expect for your boy to be dead," I respond.

"Yeah, I have to admit that I didn't expect you to be here. Sometimes things don't go as planned, but I know I'll be the last man standing," Kevin states.

"I beg to differ. You'll be leaving here just like Eric and that's dead as hell," I comment.

"I'm not gonna lie. I'm really mad as hell this didn't go the way we anticipated. We had it all worked out. We just knew the house was empty," Kevin reveals.

The shooting is paused for several moments while we talk.

"I'm not surprised that you feel that way. It makes sense that you're mad that you and Eric ended up on the wrong side of your plot. Oh, yeah about the house being empty, that was all a charade," I reply.

"But we saw you leave. We saw you take Sheena to the hospital," Kevin whispers.

"No, actually you only saw me put Sheena in the car and drive away. You heard us talk about taking her to the hospital which is exactly what I wanted you and Eric to hear," I remark.

"So, there was nothing wrong with Sheena? It was all made up? What about the poison?" Kevin inquires.

"Yes, it was all made up. Everybody was in on it. Oh, I got rid of the poison. I poured that shit out right after Eric planted it in the house. I knew I needed to keep an eye on you two. I was always one step ahead of you. I watched you guys staking out Sheena's house," I report.

"How did you know?" Kevin asks.

"Well, I guess I can tell you, since you won't be around much longer to repeat this information. The day I shot at you and Eric when you two were assaulting me, I knew you guys were trouble. I decided to have Leslie give you a call and rekindle your previous relationship. I knew you were vulnerable and would accept any affection sent your way. From that point, it was easy. You told on yourself from all the late nights of pillow talk with her. Leslie relayed all the details of your plot to me. I bet now you're realizing that she always popped up at the most convenient moments," I communicate.

"I thought she genuinely cared for me. She made me feel like I was special. I guess you can't trust a big butt and a smile for real," Kevin utters.

"No, you can't, but you did and now it's over for you. I'm sure the police won't care much about the death of you and Eric. You two are burglars who managed to get killed during the process. You guys should have been more thorough with your scheming," I say. "I have to admit that you two threw me for a loop when Sheena was attacked here."

Kevin speaks, "I guess you knew we were watching social media to see what was going on with Sheena at the hospital too. I don't know what other attack you're talking about. That must have been Eric because it wasn't me. He wanted Sheena dead with a passion."

"Of course. We played that off lovely. We knew that you guys were wall watchers and would be completely interested in what was going on. I'm sure the engagement really infuriated you. For the record, the engagement is real," I explain.

"The rest of that stuff was pure fiction."

While hiding on the floor, Kevin voices, "We really made a mess of this. I guess there's no way that I get to slide out of here like I was never here."

"I'd never be able to sleep comfortably if I did that. You'd eventually seek revenge on me and my family. The answer is no, I won't be able to look the other way on this one," I reply.

I still don't have a clear line of sight on Kevin, so I go upstairs and sneak down the back staircase that leads to the kitchen. My best bet is to try to sneak up behind him in an attempt to take him down. While I'm making my way down the back staircase, my phone chimes to alert me of an incoming message. Damn, Sheena had poor timing on this one because Kevin hears my phone chime.

"I heard your phone chime dumb ass. You should have had it on silent. You don't know how to creep obviously," Kevin speaks.

Kevin slides to another position to cover himself from me on the back staircase. I know I could have gotten him had my phone not chimed. That was a golden opportunity that I missed.

"Call it quits man. The cops will be here any minute. Throw your gun down. Just take this loss like a man," I order.

"I won't be here when they arrive. I'm getting outta here," Kevin explains.

I hear the front door open up and Sheena

calls out for me.

Kevin states, "Tonight is my lucky night. Sheena's going down if I am."

I scream, "Sheena, get the hell outta here! Run!"

Kevin fires a couple of shots in my direction and then runs for Sheena. I chase after him while firing at him. The house sounds like the Fourth of July on the Hudson. He shoots at Sheena as she tries to open the door and run back outside. Fortunately, Kevin is either a horrible shot or he's scared because he misses Sheena each time he shoots. He lunges for her and has ahold of her arm.

Finally, one of my shots hits Kevin in the shoulder and spins him around. He still has the gun in his hand, so I continue shooting at him until the clip is empty. The momentum of the shots makes him fall on Sheena. There's blood everywhere, but Kevin is dead. I walk over to his lifeless body and grab his gun. I've seen too many movies where the criminal is thought to be dead, but isn't and shoots everybody.

I pull Kevin off of Sheena and see the worst sight that I've ever seen. Sheena has been shot several times and is bleeding profusely. The shots I hit Kevin with went through him and into Sheena. What the hell? I reach in Sheena's pocket and grab her phone to call 911.

Ilesha runs in the house when she hears my calls for help. She opens the door and sees the blood bath that I've created. She breaks down crying when she notices Sheena's blood-soaked body on the floor.

"What the hell happened? Is she dead?" Ilesha asks.

"I accidentally shot her when I was shooting at Kevin. He ran after her, I shot, and hit both of them," I explain. "I checked for a pulse, but I couldn't feel one. I don't know if she's dead or not."

I tell Ilesha to go grab a towel. She runs to the bathroom to grab the towel and comes back swiftly. I instruct her to apply pressure to Sheena's wounds to help slow the bleeding. Ilesha calls out loudly for Rachel to come inside to help us out. Unfortunately, Sheena still lies motionless on the floor soaked in a puddle of blood. I can't believe that I've shot my fiancé. Rachel enters the house with the boys and sees Sheena on the floor. She releases a loud shriek and puts the boys in the living room and comes back to the foyer.

"Oh my God. My sister. You can't die. Your boys need you in their lives. You have to make it for them. Don't lose your will to live," Rachel says as she rubs Sheena's hand compassionately.

Rachel cries as she recites the Lord's Prayer. I hope help arrives soon because Sheena has lost a lot of blood. We have no idea what we're doing, but we're doing our best to comfort

Sheena and hopefully keep her alive. Apparently, we've been making a tremendous amount of noise because the neighbors are all gathered outside trying to find out what's going on, but we don't inform them. The ambulance finally arrives and storms the house to begin treating Sheena. The first responders lift Sheena onto the stretcher and hook up what seems like a million tubes to her. Rachel and Ilesha embrace one another while they cry softly. I'm not crying, but I am very upset, so I walk outside to the porch for some air.

Detective Mosely pulls up with several other cops. He talks to me for a brief moment while the other officers go in the house to start their police work.

"What happened here?" he asks.

"Go inside and you'll see what happened," I answer.

Officer Mosely goes inside the house to see exactly what I'm talking about. The scene outside is like something out of a movie or a novel. The ambulance's lights fill the air like strobe lights at a nightclub. There are also three police cars' lights that further fill the night air and make it more surreal. The street is blocked off and the onlookers have been pushed back by the police and crime scene tape is being put up.

"Is she going to make it?" Rachel asks as we follow the stretcher down the steps.

The ambulance worker responds, "It doesn't

look good. She's in a very perilous situation."

We all hoped for a more optimistic answer even though we all know that Sheena is in awful shape. We follow the ambulance to the hospital. It only takes ten minutes to get to the hospital, but it seems to take ten years. The ambulance pulls into the emergency room intake and a team of nurses and doctors meet them. They take Sheena directly into emergency surgery. Rachel, Ilesha, and I park the car and head to the waiting room. We wait to hear back from the doctor while Sheena's in surgery. We don't converse at all while we wait. I guess it's because we are all nervous and emotional. This is a very uncertain time and we really don't have anything positive to speak on. Although we don't converse, Rachel leads us in several prayers asking for Sheena's healing.

Hours later we finally see the doctor coming from down the corridor. He's only thirty feet away, but I feel like he's thirty miles away. The doctor isn't making eye contact with us as he walks in our direction.

"Why isn't he looking at us? Why would the doctor be looking at the floor and not at us directly if he had good news?" I inquire.

Ilesha says, "Hell, I don't know, but this doesn't look good y'all. He's not looking at us for a reason. Damn, I think he has bad news."

The doctor finally makes it to us and introduces himself. We don't care to hear this small talk.   All we want to know is if Sheena survived or not.

The   doctor   states,   "Ms.   Mills   sustained gunshot wounds as you already know and she lost a tremendous amount of blood. She didn't......."

Before   the   doctor   finishes   his   statement, Rachel   hears   the   words   "she   didn't"   and immediately falls into Ilesha's arms screaming. Ilesha and Rachel both embrace while they sob uncontrollably. This is crazy as hell to say the least.

EPILOGUE

I know many of you are mad that I was complicit in the deaths of Kevin and Eric. I totally understand your anger and I understand if you don't like me very much. That's okay with me. I don't apologize for my actions because I did what I had to do. I had to do what I had to do for my boys, Sheena, and myself. I was not raised to be the victim and I chose not to be victimized by Kevin and Eric. It was either them or them harm us. I never intended for Sheena to be hurt in my process to protect my family, but in war there is often collateral damage. I hope you choose your personal welfare over someone who tries to hurt you. Ladies, if he's trying to hurt you emotionally, you should leave him. If he's tries to physically harm you, you should harm him before he gets you. Sometimes love ducks and dodges you, but if it's true love, it'll find its way to your doorstep. Be confident because there is somebody out there for everyone.

www.ingramcontent.com/pod-product-compliance
Lightning Source LLC
Chambersburg PA
CBHW070116260626
47160CB00004B/1497